She didn't move. He hardly dared to breathe. A midnight silence lay upon the land around them. They were facing each other, his arms about her. Slowly, her arms came around him too and she said in a voice that was quiet as the movement of a mouse through the summer grass, "I love you, Rick."

He leaned down to kiss her, touching his lips to hers tentatively as, far off across the fields, an owl hooted and a warm wind brought the smell of apple blossoms from the orchard.

Dear Readers,

We at Silhouette would like to thank all our readers for your many enthusiastic letters. In direct response to your encouragement, we are now publishing *four* FIRST LOVEs every month.

As always FIRST LOVEs are written especially for and about you—your hopes, your dreams, your ambitions.

Please continue to share your suggestions and comments with us; they play an important part in our pleasing you.

I invite you to write to us at the address below:

Nancy Jackson
Senior Editor
Silhouette Books
P.O. Box 769
New York, N.Y. 10019

MORE THAN FRIENDS
Becky Stuart

First Love from Silhouette

Published by Silhouette Books New York

America's Publisher of Contemporary Romance

SILHOUETTE BOOKS, a Division of Simon & Schuster, Inc.
1230 Avenue of the Americas, New York, N.Y. 10020

Copyright © 1983 by S. Buchan

Distributed by Pocket Books

ISBN: 0-671-53370-3

First Silhouette Books printing November, 1983

10 9 8 7 6 5 4 3 2 1

America's Publisher of Contemporary Romance

Printed in the U.S.A.

For Thorn,
who will know why.

1

Rick Prescott watched his stepfather strap down the tarpaulin on the trailer. The house was empty now. All the heavy furniture had been sold. Most of the small pieces had gone at the garage sale. All that was left was the personal belongings of the family and what was on the trailer.

"That should do it," his stepfather said, stepping back to look over his work. "You think that will hold us to Florida?"

Rick couldn't speak for a second. He could see the empty house with the "Sold" sign in front of it behind the car, his mother getting his stepbrother, Donny, and his stepsister, Helen, organized in the back of the car for the long trip south. They were going to take shifts driving all night, hoping to make Florida from Virginia in one day. They had heard there was work down there.

"Yeah, that'll hold," Rick said. "Hey," he said, pointing to the plates on the rented trailer, "you got Florida plates already, Kenny. You're almost a native."

"Don't become a native until you pay your first taxes," Kenny said. "Let's hope we got some taxes to pay this year." The months without work had taken a heavy toll on Kenny. He was a carpenter. The recession had hit the construction business hard in southern Virginia.

Kenny held out his rough hand. "Well, Rick, I guess this is it for a while."

Rick could feel the calluses under his handshake. "Thanks for the hundred dollars, Kenny," he said. "I know it means a lot to you."

Kenny looked embarrassed. He was a big man, heavy, but underneath he was as gentle as a rabbit. "Wish it could be more," he said. He looked away, past Rick, at the house. "Heck, I wish you were coming with us."

"No, I'm doing the right thing," Rick said. "I've got to finish high school. Might as well stay and do it now and get it over with."

Kenny was a good man, and Rick knew there was more he wanted to say, but he couldn't find the words. "Yeah, I guess you're right," he said. "Wish I had finished high school. You do more than that, son. You get yourself a full education. Nobody can ever take that away from you."

Kenny turned away quickly and went to the front of the car. He got inside and turned to talk to the two younger children in the back. Rick's mother came over. Rick put his arm around her. "If you cry, I'm going to cry," he told her, making a joke of it. "What sort of an example would that be?"

"Oh, honey," his mom said, leaning her head against him. Rick could remember the exact day he realized he was as tall as his mother. He was thirteen, and they had just moved into this house. Now Rick, at five eleven, was a good five inches taller than his mother and still growing. "I'm going to miss you."

"I'm going to miss you too," he told her. "But I've got a job and a place to stay, and the next time you see me, I'll have a high school diploma."

His mom nodded miserably, as though he had just told her that the next time she saw him, he'd have mumps. "I love you," she said.

"And I love you, too," he told her.

She searched his face for some sign that would reassure her he would be all right.

"Now you go off to Florida," he told her, holding her by both shoulders.

His mom hugged him hard. "You've always

got a home with us," she told him seriously.
"You know that."

He nodded. "Now go on," he told her, "or
Florida might blow away in a hurricane before
you get there."

"Can we give you a lift to Adele's?" his mom
asked as he led her to the car. Kenny had the
engine running.

"No," he said. "All my stuff's there already.
I've got to go check my shift at the garage. I was
lucky to get the job. I don't want to be late."

He helped his mom into the car. Kenny
leaned over. "We'll call tomorrow night," he
said.

Now Rick knew his mom was going to cry, so
he kissed her fast; he closed the car door,
stepped back and waved. Kenny took the hint.
He stepped on the gas, and the old white
Pontiac lumbered slowly on down the drive,
with Donny and Helen waving through the back
window. Rick stood there a while longer by
himself, listening to the silence. He could hear
the trees rubbing their branches against each
other, and he could hear the creek at the far end
of the property, and in his mind he could hear
the echoes of other times, the better times,
when Kenny had regular work and they'd
bought this house, birthdays and Christmases,
the best years of his growing up.

A whole part of his life was over, Rick knew.
Kenny and his mom and the two younger

children had their life together now, and Rick had his.

He took a deep breath, shook his heavy blond curls and blinked up into the spring sunlight. He shrugged. Time to get on with his life.

2

Rick heard the car coming at a great speed while it was still a long way off. Sometimes Rick could identify cars by their engines. He could tell a pickup truck by the deeper growl of the motor, a four-passenger family special by the steady, untuned motor, or Harley's bucket of bolts by its smooth engine, worked on free and regularly by Rick in return for rides to school.

But this car had a high, fine-tuned motor Rick had never heard around here, smooth but angry, with a stick shift that whoever was driving was working badly, not quite meshing the clutch with the change of gears. Ahead, the road, potted with holes from the winter's snow and ice, snaked through the budding spring countryside. The spring runoff from the creek had begun, and a sheen of water lay across parts of the road.

Rick wouldn't turn around. If he turned around, it would look as though he were asking for a ride. If it was someone who knew him who had the time, they would stop. The car took the curve behind him in third gear, ground down into second, and sent out a roar as the driver lost control for a minute. Rick turned quickly to see a red sports car a quarter mile back where the road turned with a dark-haired driver fighting for control. The car skidded sideways toward the drainage ditch, which was filled with muddy water, spun around in a circle, wobbled back and forth, the driver spinning the wheel fast to try to get control, and then shot forward on the dirt road. This close, Rick could see the driver was a girl with long, dark hair that flew in the wind as she fought the road, full lips pressed tight together in fear and eyes wide with panic. The car steadied as Rick was twenty feet away, still running, and the girl saw him for the first time, her eyes wide with a panic that turned quickly into anger, as though Rick had been spying on her.

"Hey," Rick called to her, wanting to warn her that there were other curves ahead. But she floored the accelerator defiantly and shot past him, sending up a spray of mud and dirty water that hit Rick full in the face and drenched his body as surely as though he had thrown himself into the ditch.

Shocked speechless, Rick stood where he was with his mouth open and the taste of mud on his tongue as the car took the next curve without slowing down, ground the gears again and flew on.

"Moron," Rick muttered as he heard the sound of the red sports car's motor die away in the distance. He looked down at his shirt, now covered with mud spots, and at his clean jeans, stained with dirty water. Terrific impression he was going to make turning up for his first shift filthy dirty. Heaving with anger, he trudged on along the lane. Even the sight of the spring buds on the linden trees didn't break his black mood, nor the rolling hills of fresh spring grass that he loved, the split-wood fences separating proper- ties holding to the contours of the hills as they rolled away in the distance. A colt ran in a field on a far hillside, throwing its young head proud- ly high, the high, thin whinny traveling through the clear air of the afternoon while its mother watched from under a tree. Smoke rose from behind a stand of oak trees, still bare enough of leaves to show a big white house standing on its own acres of garden. One day, he would own land like this with a nice house and horses, Rick promised himself.

And one day he'd find that girl who had

covered him in mud and wring her city neck for her. Only a city person would do a thing like that, Rick thought. She didn't live around here. He hadn't recognized her; even through his anger, the image of her clear brown eyes and the long hair thrown across her shoulder by the movement of the car came back to him suddenly, and he had another sensation, not quite anger but something like it, that made his heart sort of constrict, take an extra beat, and run on, furious again. She had a face like someone you see on television, Rick thought, wide-browed, perfect skin, tanned very slightly, her eyes set evenly over a straight, determined nose. Only her lips gave her away; they turned down slightly at the corners as though nothing were ever quite right. Spoiled brat, Rick decided.

He heard the sound of another, well-known engine, and this time he stopped and waited.

"Let me compliment you on your wardrobe," Harley said, pulling his falling-apart twelve-year-old Buick convertible to a slow stop beside Rick. Harley was Rick's best friend. They were both loners. "No matter what you throw on, you always look as though you stepped right out of a fashion magazine."

"Stuff it, Harley," Rick said, going around and getting in the passenger seat. The old Buick was a bucket of bolts, paint peeling, rusted, the seat cover torn, but the engine that Rick had worked on was in perfect tune.

"Swim around here often?" Harley said, moving off.

"Some bird brain in a red sports car came by like the Indy Five Hundred. Almost put herself in a ditch, then looked at me like I had been personally responsible for it and lead-footed the accelerator. Probably find her around one of these corners wrapped around a tree."

Harley said, "I went over to the house looking for you."

"They left about an hour ago," Rick said.

Harley drove for a while without talking. "How you feeling?" he asked finally.

Lonely was the word that came to mind. But men weren't lonely, Rick reminded himself, and besides, it might offend Harley. "Okay," he said.

"What time you get off?" Harley asked.

Rick shrugged. He felt the wet shirt stick against his skin. "Will you look at this," he said, pulling the checked flannel shirt away from his skin. "What are they going to think of me, turning up like some catfish that's been lying in the mud all day."

"They're hiring you to fix up cars," Harley said, "not to dress up. Wouldn't think they'd care. I'll come around and get you later if you want."

Rick squinted into the sun. Up ahead, on the edge of Manassas, visible for as far as the eye could see, was a sign in lights, UNCLE TOOTS'

CARNIVAL OF CARS, and in smaller lights below, Open for business 24 hours a day. "I don't know what time I'll get off," Rick said. "They told me to turn up today at four and I'd get my shift then."

Harley pulled to a stop at the entrance to the dealership. "One mechanic duly delivered," he said.

Rick got out. "Thanks," he said.

"Call if you need a ride," Harley said.

Rick watched Harley leave. He felt like a pig as he trudged on into the dealership. A brightly smiling young woman behind a desk right inside the showroom looked him up and down as he went in.

"I had an accident," he explained.

She ignored that. "What can I do for you?" she asked.

"I'm Rick Prescott. I'm meant to start work in the auto shop today."

She looked at a list on her desk. "Oh, yes," she said, flashing the smile that was as polished as the dozen cars in bright colors about the floor of the showroom. "Uncle Toots wants to see you first."

"He wants to see me?" Rick asked weakly.

"Uncle Toots sees all his employees personally," said the brightly dressed young woman, getting up from behind the desk. "We're like a family here. That's why he's called 'Uncle' Toots."

She led Rick back through the display of new, flashy cars in greens and gold and black and white to another office in the back of the showroom. Through the glass, Rick could see the famous Uncle Toots, recognizable from his television commercials, sitting behind his desk, working on some papers. Uncle Toots was bald, with a thick fringe of hair trimmed close above tiny ears, heavy eyebrows, and a wide mouth that was clutched tight around a dead cigar. He was a small man, and his arms, as he sat working at his desk, looked thin beneath the gray checked suit, but the hands at the end were strong, with short fingers and thick wrists.

The young woman knocked and opened the door. Uncle Toots looked up irritably. "This is Rick Prescott," she told Uncle Toots.

Uncle Toots looked at Rick as though he were about to put out a contract on his life. He didn't crack a smile or say a word.

"For auto mechanics," the young woman reminded Uncle Toots.

Uncle Toots sat back in his chair. The chair and the desk were raised one more level above the rest of the office, so Uncle Toots looked bigger. He looked Rick up and down. "Cleanliness is next to godliness, son," he said.

"I was walking here," he said, "and some idiot out-of-state driver came around a bend too fast, hit a curve, and spun out. I got sprayed with mud."

Uncle Toots nodded as though considering whether to believe Rick or not.

He looked down at the papers on his desk. "Got your references right here somewhere," he said. He found the sheet of paper with the school's crest on the stationery and studied it for a long minute.

"Mighty impressive," Toots Shaw said, looking again at Rick's references. "Mighty impressive. You must be some fine mechanic, son, from what your teacher says here." He flipped the sheets on the desk in front of him with the tip of one cigar-stained finger.

"I liked auto mechanics. I worked on it," Rick said modestly. He wasn't sure whether Toots Shaw, the owner of the biggest car dealership in the town, was really impressed or not.

"When I was a boy," Uncle Toots said, patting around in his tailor-made suit jacket for another cigar, "they didn't teach things like auto mechanics at school. They taught reading and writing and arithmetic at school." He found a fresh cigar, stripped the cellophane paper from it, and started patting his pockets again. He took out a plain box of matches and struck one. Uncle Toots drew on the cigar until the end glowed. "Now in those days," he said, "people wanted to work. There wasn't any unemployment, no welfare. You worked, or you starved."

Uncle Toots looked over the lit cigar at Rick

with small, pale eyes. Rick felt his anger rising. He thought of Kenny and all the months of no work. Kenny had been willing to do anything. Kenny had hated staying at home; he worried every day and every night as his savings dwindled and the family went into debt. Uncle Toots had forgotten an awful lot about being poor, Rick thought.

"I'm a real good mechanic, sir," Rick said steadily.

Uncle Toots puffed on his cigar twice more, studying Rick. "Don't doubt it," he said finally, but the way he said it, Rick knew he did. "Fact is, however, that I've got no choice. No one wants to work the night shift, anyhow. People want to be home at night, so you're what I've got."

Rick wanted to reach over the desk, lift Uncle Toots off his thin behind and shake him until the cigar dropped out of his mouth. But what he did instead was say, "I appreciate you giving me the chance. It means a lot to me, you giving me this job. I hope to be a self-made man myself someday. I need this job to go to school." Every word seemed to stick in his throat as he said it, but he said it.

Uncle Toots flushed. Rick wasn't sure whether he was pleased or still human enough to be embarrassed. "Yes, yes," he said, standing up. On his feet, he barely reached Rick's shoulder. From where Rick stood, he could look right down on Uncle Toots' bald head. "A fine attitude," Uncle Toots said. "Attitude—that's what's important, boy. A man's attitude determines his destiny," he said. "If you think success, you'll be a success. Think failure, you'll be a failure. Ask me; I know. I'm a success."

"Yes, sir," Rick said, not allowing his true feelings to show. "No one could deny that looking around here."

Uncle Toots accepted the compliment as no more than right. He slapped Rick on the shoulder. "Good boy," he said. "I like to meet every new employee myself. Makes it like a family."

"Come on," Uncle Toots was saying. "I'll take you and introduce you to the head night mechanic. Twenty-four hours a day. That's our motto at 'Uncle Toots' Carnival of Cars.' Twenty-four hours a day. You can buy a car from Uncle Toots at any hour of the night or day."

"Yes, sir," Rick agreed. "I've seen your commercials."

"Everybody's seen my commercials," Uncle Toots said, strutting on ahead of Rick through the showroom. "I'm the single biggest advertiser locally."

Uncle Toots went on through the showroom and out a side door. Rick followed him and found himself in the auto-body section of the dealership. He smelled the grease from the hydraulic lifts. Cars in different states of disassembly sat at evenly spaced pits along the length of the shop except the last while teams of mechanics worked on them. "Twenty-four hours a day," Uncle Toots said with satisfaction."

Rick followed him along the length of the room until they came to a small, dirty office with a sign *Ben Black* outside. The man inside was huge, the biggest man Rick thought he had ever seen, and all muscle. He wore grease-stained overalls. His hands were black with oil.

"Why's the last pit empty," Uncle Toots greeted him, going in. "Empty pit makes no money, Ben." He tried to make it a joke, but it was no joke. Uncle Toots meant what he was saying.

"Neal's car has to be put up," Ben said, looking up from his manual. "Trying to figure out if we've got the parts."

"Neal?" said Uncle Toots. As he said it, his voice changed from the aggressive, half-whining tone he used in his usual speech to something softer. "Neal's here?"

"Came in twenty minutes ago."

"Where is she?" Uncle Toots said.

"Out back. Tore something off the undercarriage on a back road."

Uncle Toots looked at Rick as though he had no idea at all who he was. Uncle Toots faltered. "This is . . ."

"Rick Prescott," Rick said.

"Welcome," Ben said. "I've got you on the four to midnight. That okay?"

"Course it's okay," Uncle Toots said.

But Ben waited for Rick to nod and say, "Thanks, that'll work out fine."

"Overalls over there," Toots said, pointing to a pile of clean overalls. "Might as well get to work right away. We've wasted enough time as it is. Why didn't you tell me Neal was here?" he demanded of Ben.

"She didn't ask me to. She wants the car fixed by tonight," he said. "I told her I'd see if we could. She's waiting."

Uncle Toots hurried out the small, closed-in office. Ben said to Rick, "Don't pay him any attention. His bite is worse than his bark."

Rick laughed. "What's the car?" he asked.

"Foreign," Ben said. "She drives it too fast and too rough. Not safe for man or beast on the road with her free."

Rick felt the hair on the nape of his neck rise. *He knew without asking whose car was out there.*

"Still," Ben was saying, "when the boss's daughter wants her car by eight, the boss's daughter gets it if it's humanly possible." He went back to the manual.

Rick went over to the pile of clean overalls. His stomach felt as though it had dropped away from within. He felt as though he'd had his own transmission torn out. "This is stupid," he told

himself. "This is dumb." He held up one pair
after another of blue overalls with the legend
"Uncle Toots' Carnival of Cars" sewn in red on
the pocket until he found a pair that were long
enough. "Where can I change?" he asked.

Ben pointed to a row of lockers across the
garage in another room with the door open.
Rick went over there, stripped off his wet,
mud-stained clothes and pulled on the overalls
over his underwear. The cloth of the overalls
stretched across his heavy shoulders, but by
bending slightly, he could zip them up.

"You make any sense of this?" Ben asked,
pushing the manual over to Rick when he went
back to the office. The illustration was clear,
but the instructions were in German. Rick
laughed. "I had one semester of German," he
said. "Not enough to fix a car."

Together, Rick and Ben studied the manual,
trying to identify in German which each of the
illustrated parts were. They were about to give
up when Uncle Toots hurried back into the
office. "Come on, come on," he said. "Neal's
getting cold out there waiting."

The look Ben shot Uncle Toots would have
sent a more observant man running. Ben got
up. "Let's get her up on the lift," he said.

Rick followed Ben out of the garage. The
spring twilight was falling as they came out into
the open. Neal Shaw stood against the red
sports car, her arms crossed. "I don't know

what's wrong," she was saying as Ben approached, with Rick behind him. "But it makes this awful sound when I shift." Her voice was soft, much lower than Rick had expected, and almost apologetic. Ben stopped a few feet away from the car, and Rick stepped forward to get a better look at it. As he did so, Neal Shaw pushed herself away from the car to get out of the way, and they collided. Rick reached out and grasped her shoulders to steady her. They both stood exactly where they were, unmoving, and Rick felt a power flow through him that was both excitement and nausea. He could feel Neal's shoulders under his hands the way he had never touched anyone before in his life.

"What are you doing?" Uncle Toots' voice said loudly behind Rick. Rick dropped his hands. Neal didn't move. She stood as though rooted like a linden tree to the blacktop.

Then the moment passed, and Rick said quickly, "I'm sorry."

"You should watch where you're going," Uncle Toots said.

"It was my fault," Neal said. She hadn't taken her eyes off Rick's face since she collided with him.

"Now what about the car?" Uncle Toots said. "Can it be done by tonight? Neal needs it tonight."

"The car doesn't matter," Neal said dully.

"What? I thought you wanted it for tonight. I

thought you were driving over to have dinner with Brad and his parents."

"I'll take one of the other cars, daddy," she said. Suddenly, she shivered. "I'm cold, daddy," she said.

The night was falling fast. Shadows crept across the blacktop. A wind was coming up. In the first pale shadow of the evening, Rick thought Neal Shaw was the most beautiful girl he had ever seen. Out of the car, she was almost as tall as he was. The green of her silk blouse brought out flecks of gold in the depths of her brown eyes; they swept once more over Rick as she leaned into the car and took out her handbag. "Let's go, daddy," she said softly.

Rick watched them walk together across the lot, the short, stuttering father and the graceful, tall daughter, and one clear thought went through his mind: *How could a toad like Uncle Toots be the father of a beauty like Neal?*

3

Everything that could go wrong went wrong from that moment on. Rick could see Ben Black looking at him as though he had forgotten those references. When Ben asked for a wrench, Rick handed him a hammer. When he asked Rick to drain the oil pan, Rick stared up into the underbody of the car as if he were looking at the stars and had never seen the night before. He felt like a complete fool, and he knew why; he couldn't get Neal Shaw out of his mind.

"Come on, Prescott," Ben shouted at him. "Take her down. That's the best we can do for the night."

They had worked on Neal's car straight through. He pushed the button to lower the red car down to floor level. She certainly had a beautiful car, Rick thought. He wondered what a car like that would cost, what it would be like to be able to buy anything you wanted. What he wanted was to be able to make a decent living all his life and maybe help his mom and Kenny if they ever needed it.

The red sports car sat arrogantly alone amid the other half-fixed cars. "Take her out," Ben said, throwing the keys to Rick.

"Where?" Rick asked, shocked.

"Take her out onto the lot," Ben said. "You heard what Toots said. An empty bay makes no money. And when you've done that, you can go home. That's enough for one night."

That's enough incompetence for one night, Rick thought. He couldn't apologize to Ben. What could he say. Ben I'm really not like this. I'm really a very together guy, but you see I've had this little problem all night. I haven't been able to get the sight of Neal Shaw out of my mind for four hours.

Rick approached the sports car. He'd never ridden in anything so expensive. He felt suddenly very shy, as though the car knew it. He went and got a towel from the locker room and put it over the black leather seat before he opened the door and slid in behind the wheel. The car smelled of good leather. He touched the wheel reverently. The steering wheel was hand-carved wood. When he closed the door, the only sound was a sigh.

Rick made sure the brake was on, put the car in neutral, and turned on the engine. A soft purring filled the interior. He pulled on the switch for the lights, sending two piercing beams forward against the back of the shop. Ben came out of the office, pressed a button on the wall, and the rear door started to lift with a whine. Rick released the brake, put the car into reverse and turned to watch the rear as he backed out. The sports car slid smoothly out of the well-lit garage into the night. Another car was already waiting with a lot boy behind the wheel. The boy drove the car into the garage, and the door descended.

Rick was alone out on the back of the lot with the red sports car. *Neal's sports car.* He sat there with both hands on the wheel, thinking about that. She rode around in this car every day. She drove this car every day. This car was part of her world. Her clothes, her room, her house, everywhere she went, were like this car—the best, smooth, perfect.

Like Neal, he thought. Then he thought, Prescott, you jerk. Get real.

He drove the car across the lot to where it would be safe, where no other car doors being opened carelessly could chip its perfect paint, turned off the engine, put the car in gear and pulled on the hand brake. The last thing he did was turn off the headlights, plunging the whole corner of the rear lot into darkness.

He was exhausted.

I would like to sleep here, he thought. I could just slide down a bit and go to sleep on these leather seats. The thought of the long hitch to Linden made his eyelids feel a hundred pounds heavier and his bones weary. He forced himself to get out of the car. With the lights off, the car itself seemed to have fallen into a contented sleep. Rick patted the fender tenderly. "Lucky beast," he said aloud. "You get to carry her around every day."

He went back into the building. He threw the dirty overalls and the towel he'd used to sit on in the car into the laundry hamper in the corner of the locker room and distastefully pulled on his own dirty clothes. Harley was waiting as he came out. "Hi ya, buddy," Harley said. "Slide in."

"I thank you," Rick said, doing as he was told. "But what in the name of all that's decent are you doing out here at this time of night?" He closed his eyes. The next thing he knew, Harley was turning into the driveway of the house where he lived with his mother, Adele. The house was in darkness as they went in. Harley said, "Your bed's made up. I would suggest you take a shower, old buddy, unless you want Adele on your neck when she sees the sheets." Harley went off to his own room and closed the door. Harley was the only guy Rick knew who called his mother by her first name. Rick called Kenny by his first name, but Kenny was his stepfather.

Rick took a shower, found his pajamas in the bottom of the suitcase that he had brought over earlier and climbed between the sheets of the narrow bed in the small spare room. He had one last thought of his mom and Kenny and the two younger children somewhere south on the highway, then a quick picture of Neal's face as he had first seen it when the car skidded past him almost into the ditch, the wide eyes that had first seemed filled with panic, then suddenly anger, and the stubborn mouth and straight nose, and he was asleep.

"Toots Shaw," Adele said the next morning at breakfast. "I've known Toots Shaw since he was dealing in stolen cars."

"Times have changed," Harley said. Harley was the one making the breakfast. Harley did most of the chores around the house. Adele's beauty parlor supported them.

"Times may change," Adele said, "but people don't. What you are when you're twenty, you are when you're forty."

Harley said, "People change every day."

Harley dropped the eggs into the pan and scrambled them with a fork. "Rick," he said, "you're in charge of the toast."

Rick got up and went to the counter. He dropped two pieces of bread in the toaster and waited.

"So how was the first night?" Adele asked.

"Tiring," Rick admitted.

"You'll get used to it," Adele said sympathetically. "When I first opened the beauty parlor, I thought my legs would drop off from standing on my feet all day. Now I barely notice it."

"I thought I could fall asleep in a car out there," Rick admitted.

"You did," Harley said. "Mine."

"No, I mean one on the lot. I took Neal Shaw's car out of the garage to park it on the lot, and I tell you the truth, I thought of sleeping a few hours before I hitched back here."

Adele sat up straight. "Neal Shaw is home?"

"Yeah," Rick said. "She's the one who got all the mud on me."

"What does she look like?" Adele asked. He knew what he wanted to say. He wanted to say she's the type of girl that once you've seen you can't stop thinking about. Instead, he said, "Okay."

"Okay," Adele repeated. "Harley, did I hear right? Did I ask Rick what the daughter of the second richest man in Linden looks like after she's been away at a boarding school for nearly eight years, and he answers, 'Okay.'"

"You heard right. The man said she was okay," Harley responded.

"Will you tell Rick," she asked her son reasonably, "having lived with your mother for nearly seventeen years, that 'Okay' is not a satisfactory answer to a question like that. In fact, 'Okay' could drive her screaming mad into the street with raving curiosity."

"You hear the lady?" Harley asked Rick.

"I heard her. She's tall," Rick offered.

"How tall?" Adele asked.

Harley came and sat down between them. He put his own plate on the table and started eating, casting curious sideways glances at Rick as he spoke.

"Shorter than I am, but not much. Five eight, maybe."

"Her mother was tall," Adele said. "A girl from D.C."

"And she's got brown hair. Long brown hair," Rick added hastily as Adele opened her mouth to demand more details. "Long, straight brown hair parted on one side."

"What was she wearing?" Adele asked, going back to her original interest. Rick told her. Adele thought about that. She thought about any other details she might have forgotten. "What color eyes does she have?" she asked finally.

"Hazel," Rick said, "with gold flecks in the depths."

There was an awful silence for a long moment. Adele stared at Rick. Harley stopped eating, his fork halfway to his mouth. They looked at each other, and then, together, as though perfectly rehearsed, they repeated to Rick, "Hazel with brown flecks in the depths."

Rick felt himself blushing crimson. "Brown," he said. "Brown—that's the color of her eyes. I just said that as a joke."

Harley turned to Adele. "Hazel," he said.

"With brown flecks in the depths," Adele told him.

Then she looked at Rick. "Oh, you poor boy," she said. "You're in love, for sure."

4

Rick worked harder than he had ever worked in his life, but still he couldn't forget Neal. She came into Uncle Toots' almost every day to see her father. She never spoke to Rick. If he was standing outside when she came, she always looked toward the garages where the mechanics were working. When she did, Rick would get that same feeling he got the first time he touched her, part excitement, part distress. She never smiled at him, never waved, never gave any indication that she really saw him, but she always looked. No matter what he was doing, Rick could hear the red sports-car engine before it arrived at the car dealership and could contrive to be outside when she drove in.

The worst days were the days when she

35

arrived with Brad Rawson. Brad Rawson seemed to have everything in the world. He was tall, broad-shouldered, with thick dark hair and an easy smile. He wasn't the tops in the smarts department, but he didn't have to be. His father owned the biggest dairy farm in Virginia. And Brad didn't put himself out to make good grades. He scraped by near the bottom, but scraped by. He had plenty of time to go out for football, basketball and baseball. If they came in Brad's car, Rick would stay inside. The sight of Brad Rawson with Neal made Rick feel worse than anything he could remember. He began to understand what poets meant about being lovesick. When he saw the two of them together, Neal and Brad, nothing seemed to have any importance. His work, school, the future—all of it paled.

He seriously thought of giving up school and work and following Kenny and his mom to Florida, but he knew that was ridiculous. He'd heard from Kenny and his mom by letter. His mom wrote that Kenny had a job, that they had an apartment, and that the weather was nice. He knew she probably missed her friends and her house.

He wrote back and told her that he was doing okay in school, that the job was fine, and that living with Adele and Harley was nice.

But he didn't write a word about Neal Shaw.

Adele reported at breakfast on Sunday that

everyone who came into the beauty parlor took it for granted that Toots had brought Neal home from boarding school to marry Brad Rawson. "He has two years of agricultural college ahead," Adele said, "and the word is Toots got worried that he might meet someone else, so he brought Neal home. She won't need an education, anyway. She's going to be so rich, and Brad, too, for that matter."

Rick felt the food stick in his throat.

He took his coat from the rack behind the kitchen door and went out into the late-spring day. He loved the country. He loved the small flowers that you only saw if you looked hard, the violets and primroses that trimmed the fields. He loved them as he loved . . . He admitted it to himself. He loved them as he loved Neal Shaw.

After that, he sat down in the shelter of the split-log fence he had been about to climb and leaned back to let the warm sun fall on his face. How could you love someone you didn't even know? How could you love someone that you've never spoken a direct word to? How could you love someone who might not even like you, let alone love you, if she knew you? And if this was love, why did it feel so terrible? Love was meant to be one of the great experiences in life.

The hot late-spring sun felt good on his skin. He was tired. Soon he drifted off to sleep.

When he awoke, the night was filled with stars, and a thin crescent moon burned silver above the land. He was shivering with cold. He got up, stretching his cramped muscles, and stumbled from the field onto the highway. His watch had stopped. He had no idea what time it was. He started out back to town through the cool night. With the falling of night came the other sounds of the country that he loved—a hooting of an owl far off, the rustle nearby of a small animal pulling farther back into cover as he passed.

At first, he thought his ears were playing tricks on him. Both cars—the red sports car and the black Charger—were tearing down the highway behind him. The cars drew closer, the sound much louder, and Rick stepped off the highway and turned just as the four headlights—the square foreign lights of the sports car and the gleaming gold ones of the Charger—topped the ridge side by side. He had to be out of his mind, Rick thought. The yellow headlights were in the wrong lane. He was passing her on a hill. Rick could hear that the two drivers were fighting. "Pull over," Brad was demanding. "Pull over!"

She was shouting back, "Get away from me; just get away from me."

The cars were much closer, almost abreast of Rick. The beams of the square headlights pinned him against the backdrop of trees and fields. The near car slammed on its brakes, and the Charger went careening on past. The brakes cried out, and the car came to a shuddering halt a dozen yards down the road. Rick ran up to the car. The top was down. Neal Shaw sat shaking in the front seat, her face streaked with tears, her hands frozen on the wheel. The Charger braked farther down the road. Rick saw it was making a fast three-way turn to come back. "Take me home," Neal said. "Please," she implored Rick. "Take me home. He's crazy."

Rick opened the door of the car to help her out, but he saw that she was cold and frightened. In one movement, he reached in, picked her up, and lifted her into the other seat. He slid in behind the wheel just as the Charger reached them.

"What do you think you're doing, Prescott?" Brad Rawson demanded from inside the black car. "That's my girl you've got there."

"Just go," Neal implored.

Rick put the sports car in gear, put his foot heavily on the accelerator and took off. "He's crazy," Neal whispered again. "He thinks he owns the world."

The sports car flew through the night under Rick's direction. The Charger came after him fast, but Rick knew cars better than anyone around, and he took the turns expertly, putting the little machine through its paces. He headed for the dealership, moving fast through the outskirts of town.

"No, home," Neal said, her voice stronger. "You know where I live, don't you?"

Everyone knew where Toots Shaw lived. He lived in the white mansion on Linden Hill that had once been Colonel Marchand's house. Rick changed directions easily, driving carefully through town. Brad Rawson had dropped back as they approached the town, afraid, Rick thought, of making a fool of himself in front of people who knew him.

Soon they were in country again, smooth lawns and fields and large houses spaced far apart, visible in the night only by their lights and the smoke that plumed up from their tall chimneys against the translucent, late-spring sky. Rick turned the car in at the gates through which he had never expected to drive and followed the winding driveway up through the spreading oak trees until the house came into view. He had never seen anything so large. Beautifully proportioned, the house was white, with a square central block two stories tall and two smaller wings of a single story stretching out on either side. Every window was lit as though the cost of electricity were of no importance. He pulled the car up in front of the double doors flanked by brass carriage lamps and cut the engine.

Neal made no move to get out of the car. "Are you all right?" he asked her quietly.

Now she looked at him, turning her face slightly so that her large dark eyes flashed at him from below as though she were afraid to face him. She didn't answer his question. "I don't want to go in right now," she said. "But if I sit here, someone will come out. Would you take a walk with me?"

Rick felt his throat close. He thought he wouldn't be able to answer her. Just as the silence got to the embarrassing stage, he opened the door and went around the car to help her out. Behind him, he heard the front door open and then, a minute later, as Neal took his arm and turned away from the door toward the garden, close again.

"Did you ever just want to be alone?" she asked him as she led him through an arch of greenery into a formal garden that sloped to a rise with a view of the countryside. "No, no I don't mean that as it sounds," she said, squeezing his arm. "I mean, I'm never alone. I've been at school for years and years, and daddy used to come and take me away for vacations, but I wasn't alone then. And when I came home for Christmas, there were always plenty of people in the house—the maid, the cook, and now . . ."

Rick could feel Neal Shaw's arm where it rested on his, and he could see the countryside he loved, and behind was probably the most beautiful house in Virginia. If this was a dream, he didn't ever want to wake up. Neal took her arm away from his. "Do you ever speak?" she asked him, but kindly, softly.

"I've been alone a lot," he said. "I don't mind it. I like it. But sometimes . . ."

He had been about to say that sometimes he wished he had someone to share things with, not just anyone, someone special, someone like her. In the dark, he felt himself flush with the embarrassment of what she might have said if he had spoken his mind. Yet, at the same time, he felt comfortable with her the way he had never felt comfortable with anyone else that he could remember.

The moment was broken by a voice familiar to most of the county. "Neal! Neal, where are you?"

Toots Shaw came into the garden. He stopped dead at the sight of Rick Prescott with his daughter. "Neal," he said, as though he didn't believe his own eyes.

"This is . . ." She didn't know his name, but she reached out again and touched Rick on the arm to give him support.

"Rick Prescott," Rick said.

"I know who you are," Uncle Toots said, looking up at Rick and his daughter. "What are you doing here?" he asked directly.

Neal took a firmer hold on Rick's arm. "Rick's here to have dinner with us," she said.

Even in the dark, Uncle Toots looked as though he were about to have a stroke.

Rick said, looking at Neal with thanks, "I can't, really."

"Why?" she asked him.

"Because he has to work," Uncle Toots answered for him.

That got Rick's back up. "No, I don't," he said. "It's Sunday. I could stay," he said, turning again to Neal, "if you really want me to."

"Don't make the boy do anything he doesn't want to do," her father told her.

That decided Rick. "I'd love to stay," he said.

"That's settled, then," Neal said, dragging Rick with her. She leaned over and kissed her father. "Rick drove me home," she said. "I had some trouble."

"What sort of trouble," her father asked, pushing in between Neal and Rick. Neal let Rick's arm go with a conspiratorial smile over her father's head.

"Car trouble," she said after they had walked a few steps.

"Where was Brad?" her father asked. They were nearly at the house now. From close up to the huge mansion on, Rick wished he hadn't accepted Neal's invitation. He'd never been inside anything this large that wasn't a hotel.

"He was racing around somewhere," Neal said. She said it lightly enough, but her soft voice dropped an octave as the memory came back. She led them up the steps and in through the wide double doors of the house.

The light was the first impression that struck Rick. Overhead, a bright chandelier draped in hundreds of crystal lengths bathed everything in a golden flow—the sweeping staircase, the blue carpet, the mirrors that reflected the flowers, arranged so perfectly in the huge silver urn on the polished table in the center of the hall. On either side, doors opened onto rooms such as Rick had never expected to see—a living room three times as long as any Rick had ever seen before and where only one door was open, he could see the end of a delicate formal dining table.

Neal threw her hair back over her shoulder, and chin raised, looked up at Rick and smiled.

"Welcome to Linden Hill," she said.

Rick was glad he hadn't seen her in the full light before this. If he had seen her as beautiful as this, he wouldn't have had the courage to come in. Mind you, beside Uncle Toots, Rick was pretty sure that he fit in like a prince. Uncle Toots, in his loud check suit of brown and black squares, looked as though he'd stumbled in from a fair, or a carnival for that matter, a carnival of cars.

Uncle Toots led them into the living room. Neal said, "I'm going upstairs for a minute."

When Neal was gone, Uncle Toots and Rick

had nothing to say. Uncle Toots paced out the long living room. Finally, he said, "What happened?"

"Where?" Rick said warily.

"With Brad Rawson?"

Rick wasn't sure how much Neal meant to tell her father. He said, "They had a fight."

Uncle Toots was standing with both hands behind his back, warming himself at the fire. He said over his shoulder, "And you came along?"

Rick knew what Uncle Toots was getting at. "No," he said evenly. "I was walking along the road on my way home, and Neal came along."

Toots thought about that with his back to Rick, taking all the warmth of the fire for himself. Ignored by Uncle Toots, Rick looked about the room. He wondered once again what it was like to live in a place like this. What did you feel like inside when you woke up in a house like this, came down those stairs into the main hall, had breakfast in that big dining room and then went out to a new car? He couldn't begin to imagine what it would be like except to know that Neal and he were different, very different. He had a quick thought of Neal's trying to live in the small house where he had lived with his mom and Kenny, waiting in line in the morning for the bathroom, everybody together in the small living room at night, watching television or doing their homework. You knew almost everything about everybody in your family in a small house. In a house this size, you could be related and almost be strangers, like people who lived in the same hotel for years and never knew each other's names.

Neal came back into the room. She had brushed her hair and washed any sign of her earlier distress away from her face.

Uncle Toots looked her over the way he might look over a new-model car delivered from Detroit. "You seeing Brad later?" he asked her. Neal looked down at the carpet underfoot and whispered, "I don't think so." Her voice was softer again, not as strong or as angry as it had been earlier. The house had an effect on her, too, Rick thought.

"I hear you had a fight," Toots said.

Neal shot a look of betrayal at Rick. He wanted to answer her, but what could he say? He didn't know her well enough to say, "I didn't say anything."

"He always wants everything his own way," Neal answered.

The way Toots stood, his back to the fire, waiting for her to go on, Rick could see that answer didn't seem any less than perfectly sensible to Uncle Toots. Uncle Toots had probably wanted everything his own way all his life, also, and he'd got it for the most part.

"Brad's a good boy," Uncle Toots said to his daughter, and looked sourly at Rick.

Rick wanted to get out of there. He didn't belong in this house. He didn't belong here with these people. He came from another world, not any the less worthwhile, though Uncle Toots seemed to think so, but different. They didn't understand him in this world, and he didn't understand them.

Rick was thinking of some excuse that would let him leave when a maid dressed in a black dress appeared in the door. "Dinner is served, sir," she said.

Rick followed them on through the golden hall to the dining room. Three places were set at the long table, one at either end and one right smack in the center. "How do you talk to each other?" he joked. "By telephone?"

Neal smiled, but Toots sat down at his place at the head of the table as though he hadn't heard. Rick sighed.

"Can I take your coat, sir?" the maid asked him.

"No," Rick said quickly, thinking of his old, grayed Sunday shirt under the light jacket. "No, thanks. I'm a little cold." The dining room was about the temperature of South America, with another fire burning here.

The maid looked confused. "I could put some wood on the fire," she said.

"Leave him alone," Uncle Toots said.

The woman went out. For a long, uncomfortable moment, no one spoke. Uncle Toots sat drumming his fingers on the table, lost in some calculation of his own. Neal looked at her place setting, her hands crossed in her lap. Rick thought she was probably realizing that she had made a mistake by inviting him here.

The doors at the other end of the room opened, and the maid came back in carrying a huge salad bowl. She went first to Neal, who helped herself carefully, putting just a few leaves on the glass plate in front of her. Then the salad was taken down the table to Rick, who watched with trepidation as the gray-haired maid approached step by step. The maid reached his place and held the salad bowl out to him. He picked up the silver servers and could almost feel his hands shake as he helped himself to the salad, certain he was going to drop lettuce all over the polished table.

"Thank you," he said. He had two leaves and a slice of tomato on his plate.

"Take some more," Neal urged him.

"No, no, thank you," he said hurriedly. "I'm not really very hungry." He was starving. He hadn't eaten all day.

Uncle Toots dug into the salad bowl as though excavating for coal. Neal ate her salad quietly, while Uncle Toots stuffed his right in. "Rabbit food," he said. "Neal tells me it's good for you."

Rick tried to drag out his salad long enough to finish at about the same time as Neal, but there wasn't much you could do with two lettuce leaves and a slice of tomato.

"You should eat more," Neal told him. As though on cue, Rick's stomach rumbled loud and clear to the dining room. Rick flushed with embarrassment, and the corners of Neal's mouth twitched mischievously. The maid came back to take the salad plates away and brought clean dinner plates that she placed at each setting. Rick's heart sank—more self-service. This was like a cafeteria in a palace.

The next course was a silver platter of roast beef, sliced and steaming, surrounded by baked potatoes and carrots. Rick's mouth watered at the sight of it. Neal easily helped herself. The aromas of the beef and potatoes traveled across to him like waves of the rarest perfume.

The maid brought the platter down to Rick. He reached up eagerly for the servers. The maid tilted the platter slightly to make it easier for him to serve himself, but Rick's hands misjudged and knocked the edge of the platter. A look of horror crossed the maid's face as the silver platter started to slide forward. Rick saw it all as though someone had slowed down a film—the platter sliding out of the maid's outstretched hands, the meat and the potatoes tumbling forward; then, as the film speeded up, a shower of meat, carrots, potatoes, poured off the falling silver platter onto Rick, the table, the carpet, all drenched with the gravy.

No one said a word. They looked stricken as the meal fell all over Rick's chair. Neal, wide-eyed, stared at Rick in shock. Uncle Toots just looked at him.

Rick got up. Potatoes, carrots and meat fell out of his lap. He walked out of the dining room, through the hall, and out into the night. He started to run steadily, then faster and faster down the long driveway under the oak trees, out through the gates, down the highway, fleeing as though a pack of hounds were on his heels, his heart pounding in his chest. He ran and ran until he was alone in the countryside. Then he sat down on a rock at the side of the road, and in the darkness he cried. He hadn't cried like that since he was a kid.

5

Rick, wake up. Wake up!" Rick opened his eyes to see Adele, in her bathrobe, leaning over him, shaking him. "Quick, get up!" He had got in late last night, made himself two grilled cheese sandwiches, and gone to bed. "There's someone here to see you."

Groggily, Rick staggered out of bed.

"Put on a robe," Adele said.

"I don't have one," Rick told her. "Who is it?"

Adele stood back to let the full force of the announcement hit him. "Neal Shaw."

For a moment, Rick felt nothing—neither panic nor embarrassment—nothing at all. "For me?" he said.

"Not for Harley or me," Adele told him. "She's waiting outside."

Rick started to undo his pajama jacket. "What are you doing?" Adele asked.

"Putting on some clothes," Rick told her.

"She's waiting!" Adele said.

"Tell her I'll be right out," Rick said dully.

He looked around his room for something to wear. Last night's clothes lay on the floor, the gravy stains visible on the shirt and jeans. Rick opened his closet; he had a big choice—a sweatshirt that was clean and neat, which had once been navy blue and now was almost gray, a white shirt he wore with his one sports jacket or a yellow tennis shirt. He had a choice of two pairs of jeans, an old pair of beige corduroys and his gray dress slacks. He pulled on clean jeans and the yellow tennis shirt, clean socks and loafers. He went into the bathroom, washed his face and cleaned his teeth. He looked okay. What did it matter, anyway? He went out into the kitchen where Harley was standing at the stove turning bacon. "Big time, huh?" he said.

Rick didn't reply. He went outside. Neal was sitting patiently behind the wheel of the red sports car. "Hi," he said.

"Hi."

They stared at each other for a few seconds. She had her hair tied back and lifted up and pinned behind her head today. It showed off the symmetrical lines of her face but made her look more mature, also. "I don't know what to say," she said.

Rick didn't want to look at her. When he looked at her, he could feel the same far-off feeling that he had the first time he saw her up close and last night coming through the fields. He had told himself he wouldn't feel that anymore. He wouldn't allow himself to feel that. It wasn't good for him; it wasn't good for either of them. He had things to do with his life, and she had to go on with the plans for hers. They didn't belong together. There, at least, Uncle Toots was right; they came from different worlds, had different roads to follow.

"I didn't do anything," she said. "It's unfair."

"No, *I* did," he told her. "I made a jerk of myself."

"We're about even," Neal said, and Rick looked quickly enough in her direction to see the shadow of a smile pass through her gold-flecked eyes. "I throw mud on you; you throw meat and potatoes back at me."

He didn't want to, but he found he was smiling. "I didn't know you knew that you'd thrown mud at me."

"I was too embarrassed to admit it," she said. "You want to have breakfast?"

This was all wrong. He knew it. He wanted to have breakfast with Neal Shaw more than anything he had ever wanted in the world, but he knew he shouldn't. "Yeah," he said. "But then I have to go to school."

"I'll drop you there."

"Give me a minute," he asked her.

Rick went into his room and gathered his school books together. He'd taken a shower when he got home last night, and he wished he could rush through another now. He took his old sports coat out of the closet, threw it over his shoulder and went out through the front door.

"Where to?" Neal asked.

Rick directed her to a diner out on Highway 292.

She drove slowly, seemingly much more calm than he had ever seen her, but then he hadn't ever seen her in what could be described as a normal situation.

"I'm sorry about last night," she said.

"Don't be," he told her. "At least we got the worst over. You threw mud at me; I threw dinner back at you. What more could happen?" As though to warn them, they hit two hidden potholes in the highway that almost bounced both of them out of their seats. "Well, we know something else could happen, anyway," Rick said when they were back on firm ground. "So let's not tempt fate."

"You don't live at home," Neal said.

He hadn't thought until then about how she

had found out that he lived with Adele and Harley. "No, my family went to Florida."

"For the winter?" she asked.

If she'd asked him whether he was going fox hunting this weekend, the gap between them couldn't have shown wider. "You might say that," he said, and shut up.

After a while, she said calmly, but with some anger showing, "You know, I didn't choose to be rich."

He understood that. He could have said he didn't choose to be poor. So all he did was nod.

"Peace," she said.

"Peace," he agreed.

The diner was up ahead. He pointed it out to her, and she pulled off the highway and into a space between a semitrailer and a van.

They went inside and found a booth in the back. The waitress came with her pad. "Order?" she asked.

"Coffee and toast," Neal said. "I've already eaten."

"Eggs, bacon, toast, the works," Rick said. "How did you find where I lived?" he asked when the waitress was gone.

"I applied the old Chinese water torture to daddy," she said. "He wasn't thrilled."

"No, I can imagine," Rick said.

"He wants me to hook Brad Rawson and marry him," Neal said. As she said it, her mouth clenched in the same angry line that it had worn the very first day Rick saw her, the day she sprayed him with muddy water.

"What do you want to do?" he asked her.

"I don't think I really know what I want," she admitted. "I don't think I ever have."

Rick wondered then why she was home. He knew what Adele said—that Toots had brought her home to try to catch Brad Rawson—and what Neal was saying seemed to confirm it. But there were other things to think about, too. "What about school?" he asked.

"I'm finished with high school," she said. "It's different in Europe. You can write your exams early and get out early. Daddy wanted me to come home, so I did."

Their breakfast came. Rick dug into his. He realized that he was comfortable with Neal, comfortable the way he had been last night out at the rise, looking down at the rolling fields, comfortable the way he had never been with anyone and certainly never expected to be with her. She nibbled on her toast while he finished his breakfast.

"Did you know why your dad wanted you to come home?" he asked her.

"No," she said, and her mouth set once more in that stubborn look. "I thought he was lonely."

"I see," he said.

She looked out at the parking lot of the diner where the driver of the semitrailer was carefully backing his rig out of the lot. "He's not a bad man, you know," she said, and Rick knew she meant Uncle Toots. "He wants the best for me, and he's given me the best all my life, and I love him," she added with a touch of defiance.

Rick could accept that. It might be hard for anyone else to love Toots, but he could see why Neal might.

"What do you want out of life?" she asked.

He knew the answer to that one. "An education," he said.

She had no answer to that. An education had been given to her on a silver platter, and right now, Rick had enough of silver platters.

"It must be nice to know what you want," she said.

That was such a spoiled, stupid thing to say that for one brief moment Rick almost didn't like Neal. That passed right away, and he saw that beneath all that sophistication was a little girl. She might know how to check into a hotel or serve herself from a silver platter held by a servant, but she knew almost nothing about real life. "Makes things simple, I guess," he said. "Not so much knowing what you want as what you have to have to get by, what you need."

Neal held his glance, and he felt that same weakness he had felt the night he saw her on the car lot overcome him.

"What I need," Neal Shaw said, speaking directly into his eyes, "is a friend."

It was as though the bottom of the world had dropped away again. He loved Neal Shaw. But Neal Shaw was a lonely girl being pushed and pressured into decisions she wasn't ready for. The last thing she needed was another boy after her. She had spoken her needs aloud, maybe for the first time in a long time. She didn't want a boy friend. She wanted a friend. Rick knew the difference, and the difference was as wide as the two separate worlds they inhabited day by day.

He swallowed hard, trying to hide his disappointment. "You've got it," he said, and his reward was a smile that lit her face like the dawn over the Virginia hills, and then she reached out and put her hand over his. That didn't help one bit. The feel of her hand against his made it a lot worse, but he didn't say anything. He just tried a smile of his own and hoped it didn't look too sick.

He picked up the check. "My treat," he said.

"No," she said, opening her purse. "Dutch. Friends go Dutch."

"Dutch, then," he agreed. "Dutch."

6

"Your mom called," Adele said when Rick came in that night from work. He was dog-tired from his day at school and his night shift at the garage, but he felt better than he ever remembered feeling in his life. He wanted to hug Adele, dance a couple of steps, and maybe break into song. "You look like the cat that swallowed the canary," Adele said suspiciously as he put his books down on the kitchen table and went to the refrigerator to get the cheese sandwich Harley left for him every night. "It's not that Shaw girl, is it?"

Neal Shaw had driven Rick to school after breakfast, dropped him off at the walk up to the front door, and driven off, leaving Rick the most envied boy in the school. Brad Rawson and a group of his cohorts had stood around glowering at Rick as he went past them, but nobody had said anything. For one thing, Rick was pretty sure Brad Rawson didn't want to admit to anyone that he had lost his girl to Rick. He *hadn't* lost his girl to Rick, of course. Neal had made it very clear that all she wanted was a friend, but nobody else knew that.

The day had passed in a golden glow, and the work at the garage had seemed more like a reward than a chore. Neal might turn up at any time, he thought, and the hours flew. But Neal didn't come. Toots did. He came and stood in the entrance to the machine shop, unlit cigar clenched in his teeth, staring down the row of car bays in Rick's direction, but he didn't come any closer, and he didn't say anything. Rick went on working, and when he next looked casually in the direction of where Toots had been, the doorway was empty.

"I am high on life," Rick said, taking the plunge and hugging Adele.

Adele was as startled as if he had walked into the beauty parlor with a gun and held her up. She shook herself when he let her go, but she was smiling. "You *are* in love," she pronounced like a doctor making a final diagnosis. "Well, remember, love's a mixed blessing, a very mixed blessing." And with that she made her exit, pointing to the slip of paper with the long-distance telephone number on it.

Rick went over to the telephone on the wall. He asked for an operator and placed the call collect to Florida while he munched on the cheese sandwich.

The phone rang twice, and his mom picked it up. She'd been waiting for his call. The operator asked her if she would accept the charges, and from the way his mom said, "Of course," her voice filled with a laughter he hadn't heard in a long time, he knew things were fine down there in Florida.

"Hi," he said. "All tanned?"

"Will be soon," she said.

He waited. He knew his mom. When she had a secret, she liked to try and hold onto it, but every inch of her body and voice would vibrate with excitement like a little kid's, and so she never, ever could keep a secret. It was one of the family jokes that to tell mom a secret was like sending a telegram to the rest of the world that something important was up.

He let the expensive seconds drag out, smiling to himself.

"Well, aren't you ever going to ask!" his mom exploded finally.

"What?" he asked innocently.

"Rick," she shrieked down the long-distance lines, "Kenny's got a job!"

Somehow Rick had known that was what his mom's news had to be. She had phoned a couple of times before, once when they first reached Florida and were staying in a motel court and once more when they moved to a small apartment. Kenny had managed to get work right off when they got there, but it wasn't permanent work. But the sound of the excitement in his mom's voice had told Rick right away that something really good must have happened, and nothing could be as good as Kenny's having regular work. Still, the words themselves confirming Rick's suspicions had a strange effect on him. He felt his knees go weak, and a great sense of relief swept through him. The worst times were over for his mom and Kenny. Things would get better now.

"Rick?" His mom's voice had changed. "Rick, are you still there?"

Rick found he had a lump in his throat. "Yes, mom," he said quietly. "I'm still here. Mom, I'm real happy for you."

"For us," she corrected him. "For all of us. We can be together soon, Rick. You finish your school term, and we'll get settled, and we can all be together down here soon. Rick, you'll love it down here. You really will." He could hear the excitement coming back into his mom's voice. "There are oranges growing right outside the windows, and the kids have been to the beach every afternoon after school, and everybody's so nice, though nobody, almost nobody, seems to have grown up here. Everybody seems to have come from somewhere else, just like us, so you don't feel like a stranger at all. You feel just like everybody else."

"I'll bet it's real pretty," Rick said slowly. Up until this very second, he had been praying that Kenny would get a job, his mom would find them a small house, and when his school term was over, he could join them. Now, suddenly, he felt different. He still was happy for Kenny and his mom, but the thought of moving away from Linden, of moving to Florida, didn't bring the same feeling it had even a day before. Something had changed, and he was pretty sure he knew what it was.

"Oh, Rick," his mom said over the long-distance wire, "the good times are coming back. They really are. I can feel it."

"You deserve them, mom," he said. "You and Kenny deserve them more than anybody I know."

"Not just for us," his mom said. "For you, too, Rick. How are things with you?"

Rick had a flash of the good feeling he had as he walked into the house. "Great," he said, but the feeling didn't last; the uneasiness of a few seconds before returned. "Great," he said, louder.

But he had never been able to fool his mom. "You sure?" she asked.

"Positive," he told her.

"School's okay?"

"Like always," he said.

"That bad, huh?" she joked.

"Well, I've only got what I was given to work with," he teased her. "Only got the brains I inherited."

That did it. "Rick Prescott," she told him in no uncertain terms, "if I was up there this minute, I would shake you! Fact, I'll put one shake right down on a note pad for when you get down here. First I'll hug you; then I'll shake you. Right now, however, I got to get off this line before Kenny comes in here and shakes me for burning up the dollars. I'll write you all the details, honey, and you'll see; things really are turning around for all of us. Kenny would be on the line himself telling you if he weren't so tired, and I'll bet you're tired, too, so I'll let you go to bed. You be good, you hear, and it won't be long now until we're all together again." And then, after a fraction of a second's pause, she said, "Rick, we love you. We all miss you."

"I love you, too," Rick assured his mom. "You hug the kids for me and say a big hi to Kenny. 'By."

"'By." The line went dead.

Rick stood where he was, leaning against the wall, listening to the dial tone until even that changed, becoming the shrill signal that the receiver was off the hook. Why did life have to be so complicated? he thought. First Kenny had no job in Linden, and the family made plans to move, and Rick got used to the thought of going south to live in a strange place; then, when all that was just getting settled, along came Neal.

Neal.

He touched the receiver again. He wanted to pick it up and call her. He wondered what she was doing right at this minute. Was she in bed? Her bedroom probably looked like no room Rick had ever seen, no room Rick had ever imagined, the way her whole life was something magical, like something out of a story for Rick. Yet, even in that story, Neal was unhappy, too. "I need a friend," she had said. Even princesses needed friends, and in Rick's world, Neal was a princess.

And what was he? He was no prince. Brad Rawson, with his big inheritance coming, was a prince. Rick was just another working Joe who happened to be walking along a roadside when a lonely princess came by.

He took his hand off the receiver. He could just imagine the commotion on Linden Hill if he called her now—the maid and Uncle Toots and the whole household upset. He didn't even know how Neal would feel about a call this late. In some ways, he felt he knew her already better than anyone he'd ever known outside of his family, but in other ways, she was more mysterious to him than anyone had ever been. Looking at her across the breakfast table in the grubby diner, he had to make himself believe that she was really there, not something he had imagined, some apparition, the way he used to imagine things he wanted when he was very small—toys and cakes and trips to the county fair—imagining them in detail, hoping that if he wished hard enough, he would get what he wanted. Wishing that hard for something made it worse when you didn't get it—he knew that—but that was the way he was made. He had always known what he wanted, and when he knew what he wanted, he thought about that all the time, worked toward it, and hoped that if he worked hard enough and wished hard enough, he would get it. And sometimes he did. He could remember the first bicycle he had wanted and how he had delivered papers, saving up for it, and then at his birthday, when he still needed thirty dollars for it, more money than he could imagine when he was a kid, Kenny gave him the difference.

But, of course, a lot of the time he hadn't got what he wished for, and he'd learned that was just the way life was and you had to live with it.

He had been sitting there across from Neal, truly wondering if she was real or just another dream he conjured up, when she had reached over and put her hand over his. The touch of her hand had gone through him like an electric shock.

"Friends," she had reminded him before he got out of the car.

Now, as he stood in the kitchen wanting to call her, he remembered the touch of her hand as though she were right there beside him, and surreptitiously he raised his hand to see if her scent was still on it, but all he could smell was the odor of oil from the garage. That brought him down to earth hard, and he laughed aloud at his own foolishness as he turned off the kitchen light and went down the hall to his own room.

Neal rode with her back straight, the saddle firmly beneath her and her knees holding to the sides of her brown mare with assurance. Horse and rider flew out across the bright-green grass of the meadow. Rick followed on the dappled gray stallion, watching with admiration.

"This is my horse," Toots had said moments before, gingerly patting the sides of the stallion. He stood a good arm's length from the beast as he said so.

"Oh, daddy," Neal said lovingly. "You like to say that, but you know you never go near him. Porter exercises him." Porter, who stood to one side after bringing the two horses from their stalls, was the groom.

"I don't have time to ride," Toots said importantly. "You know that. I have to work so that others can ride." He glanced at Rick as he said this, but this was a weekend, and Rick had two days off. He rubbed the gray muzzle of the horse.

"Beautiful animal," he said, and the gray stallion seemed to understand him, leaning his head farther down for more rubbing.

"He never does that for anyone but Porter," Neal said musingly.

"When I was a boy . . ." Toots said, stepping carefully out of the way as the stallion did a little dance with its back feet, anxious to be out on a run. Whatever Uncle Toots had been about to announce of his youth was lost to the stallion's giving a great snort of disbelief and stepping one step toward Uncle Toots. Uncle Toots jumped back.

"That animal's dangerous," he said.

"No, he isn't, daddy," Neal said, kissing her father on the cheek. "He just wants exercise." She swung easily into her saddle, and taking the reins in her left hand, moved the mare out of the way for Rick to mount. The gray stallion was the finest horse Rick had ever seen. He took the reins, grasped the horn of the saddle, and swung up. The horse moved around in a small circle of a dance before calming down at the sure feel of Rick on his back. Rick's mom had been raised with horses, and one of the first things she had taught him was to ride. If mom could see him now, Rick thought!

With a wave of one gloved hand, Neal spurred her horse out of the yard by the stables into the lane leading to the open countryside. Toots owned all of this property, acres and acres of it, stretching green to the far horizon. Rick followed on the stallion.

"You take care!" Uncle Toots called after them as they disappeared around a bend in the lane. Neal didn't speak, she didn't turn, she didn't make any sign that Rick was with her as she led them down the lane of trees toward the open country. After that first day, he hadn't heard from her for the whole week. Each day after school he had watched for her, knowing that it wasn't likely that she would come to pick him up, and each day he had still been disappointed when he came out and saw that she hadn't come. Slowly, Harley, who had been acting strangely, relaxed and became more of his joking self again, giving Rick a lift to the garage, and twice he had been there when Rick came out after his shift to give him a ride home.

But Neal was the one Rick was watching for, and she hadn't come either to school or to the garage, not even to see her father, and slowly Rick had forced himself to realize that it was all in his own mind, the friendship, the feelings, the longings, the memory of the few minutes they had spent together, an hour at the longest. He felt pain when he finally came to understand that he had fooled himself, that when Neal had said she wanted a friend, that was all she meant. A friend was someone you waved to when you saw them across a room, someone you spent a few minutes with when you both had time, someone you went out to see a movie with on a rainy night; nothing more.

He hadn't told anybody how he felt, but he thought maybe Adele guessed from the way she looked at him as he played with his breakfast in the morning. She didn't say anything, however, and Rick turned his mind to his school work and to the work he had to do at the garage. He stopped looking at the apple-green phone on the wall, wishing it to ring, wishing he had a reason to ring her.

"Don't do this to yourself, Rick," Adele said on the Friday night when he came in from his shift. "You won't believe me when I tell you this, but a year from now, you won't even remember how you felt."

She was right. He didn't believe her. He didn't answer her, either. He wished Kenny was around. He felt he needed a man to talk to, and Harley, though he was a friend, wasn't a man yet. He took his sandwich and his glass of milk and went back to his room.

Then, in the morning, as he came out of the

house to pick up the newspaper, there she was again—Neal, sitting in her red car, waiting.

His first feeling was anger. He wanted to turn on his heel and walk back into the house. He felt he was being played with as though he were some toy or a pet or less important than she was.

He just stood and looked at her, indifferent for once that he was wearing an old, torn white T-shirt that he had slept in and a pair of baggy Levi's he'd pulled over his shorts.

"If you get mad at me," Neal said, "I'm going to cry. Everyone else is mad at me."

It took Rick a moment to find what he wanted to say, and then it was very simple. "I'm not mad at you," he said. "Not anymore."

Then neither of them seemed to know what to say next.

"You want to go riding?" Neal said finally.

Rick looked at the red car. For once, he really didn't want to drive around in that car, not with Neal at the wheel and him in the passenger seat.

"On horses," she said, as though she could read his mind.

"Yeah," he said. "I'd like that. Give me a minute to get ready." He was in the door before he realized he was being rude. He went back out again. "You want to come in?" he asked. "I may take more than a minute."

Neal got out of the car and followed him in

through the back door. Rick looked about the
kitchen surreptitiously to see what it must look
like from her eyes, but then he shrugged. This
was where he lived; this was where Adele and
Harley lived, and Adele and Harley were good
friends. He wasn't going to make any apologies
for their house.

On cue, Harley walked into the kitchen,
shuffling along in his bedroom slippers with his
old green terry-cloth robe wrapped around him.
The sight of Neal Shaw in perfectly pressed
jeans and a leather jacket that fell over her hips
stopped him cold.

"Hi," Neal said shyly.

For once, Harley was at a loss for words.
"This is my friend Harley," Rick said. "And
this is my *friend* Neal," Rick said, emphasizing
the "friend."

Harley was furious. Rick knew that look.
When Harley got furious, his head looked as
though it had been boiled in oil for an hour or
two; he seemed to swell in size and go a purple
color. "Hi," Harley muttered. Then remember-
ing himself, he said, "You want breakfast?"

"No, thank you," Neal said. "I've had breakfast."

"How about you?" Harley said, shooting
Rick a cold look.

Rick was starving. "No, thanks," he said.

"Could I have some coffee?" Neal asked.

Harley looked at her as though she had asked

for something rare and exotic. "Sure," he said grudgingly.

Rick left them there in the kitchen, thinking to himself that he didn't really mind not being the smartest guy around. Harley was the smartest guy he knew, and Harley had times when he was downright weird. Rick met Adele, wearing hair curlers, in the hall. "Neal's in the kitchen," he told her.

If he'd said the police had arrived to haul them all off for spying, he couldn't have had a greater effect on Adele. She clutched her robe to her throat, widened her eyes, and seemed to jump back. "Here?" she asked.

For one brief moment, Rick thought of saying, "No, she's in the kitchen at her own home," just to bring Adele to her senses. This whole house had gone off the tracks in the last five minutes. "Sure," he said. "Where else?"

But that was almost as galvanizing as the first announcement had been, for Adele spun around and in one leap was back in her own room with the door slammed shut. Rick stood in the hall in his bare feet, thinking that maybe people were right. People were always saying that Adele and Harley were more than just a little strange—they were downright peculiar— and Rick had always ignored that because his own mom said that people were only the way they behaved to you, not what people told you about them, and Adele and Harley had always been good to Rick. But this morning he was seeing a side of them he'd never come across before.

Rick took a quick shower, found a clean shirt, jeans, and a jacket, and went back to the kitchen. He thought he'd been fast, but what he saw there convinced him that he would never understand women. Adele, perfectly dressed and made up, was sitting having coffee with Neal. Harley was nowhere to be seen.

Neal drove in silence, and Rick had to admit it was as though they were old friends. The roads had dried, and the car moved smoothly along the back lanes toward Linden Hill. He was surprised she knew the back roads as well as she did. He said so.

"I lived here until I was eight," Neal said. "Sometimes when I was away at school, I used to imagine what it would be like to be at home again, and I'd try to remember what the house looked like and how you got to town; all of it. When I got back, I found that things hadn't changed very much."

"No," he admitted. Life didn't change very much in a small town, he knew. He supposed she was used to big cities and excitement. He loved Linden himself. When the time came to go south to join Kenny and his mom, he would miss it.

She turned the car expertly in between the

stone gateposts of Linden Hill, and they passed
up the avenue of trees toward the big white
house sprawling across the top of the hill in the
warmth of the spring sunlight. Neal drove on
past and down a narrow track through the
meadow to the stables.

Uncle Toots was standing there talking to the
groom. Neal stopped the car. She had a stubborn look on her face. She didn't get out of the
car for a few moments, and the way Toots
looked at his daughter without the usual wor-
shipful look he had when she was around, Rick
was pretty sure they had had an argument. The
groom put both his hands in his pockets and
looked at the ground.

Neal got out of the car. Rick followed. Toots
looked at Rick with cold hostility. "Hello, Mr.
Shaw," Rick said.

For a moment, Toots didn't reply. Then he
seemed to realize that his argument wasn't with
Rick but with his daughter. "Hello, Prescott,"
he muttered. Then he said to Neal, "Porter says
you want Jack and Rebel saddled."

"If it's okay with you," she said.

Toots looked at Rick. "Can you ride?"

"Yes," Rick said.

Toots turned to the groom. "Bring the horses
out, Porter," he said.

Neal said, "Thank you, daddy."

Rick could see from the way Toots looked at
Neal that under the rough, tough businessman

was another person. Rick suddenly felt closer to
Toots, as though he had an important insight
into his character.

The groom brought the horses out already
saddled. The big gray stallion snorted, rearing
his head and chomping on the bit. Toots
stepped out of the way.

"You sure you can ride that horse?" he asked
Rick.

"Yes, sir," Rick said, taking the reins from
the hands of the groom.

"And you," Toots said to his daughter.
"Maybe you should have a quieter horse."

"Jack's the quietest horse in the stable," Neal
reminded her father patiently.

"Don't worry, daddy. I promise you, I'll be
all right."

But from the way Toots had looked as Neal
and Rick rode out of the stable yard and down
the lane, Rick knew that Toots still thought of
his daughter as a very little child. Worrying
about her just came naturally, the way his mom
and Kenny worried about him.

"When I was in boarding school," Neal said,
"I used to think my father was a very tall man."
She lay on her back in the smooth grass under
an old oak tree. The sunlight through the
gnarled branches threw a lacy pattern on her
smooth skin, making her even features more
elusive than ever to catch and fix in his mind.
Faced with her there beside him on the grass,

Rick had the feeling again that she might vanish at any moment, that this must be a dream and like all dreams, he would wake. He had to smile, and Neal turned on her side and caught him. "No, I mean it," she said. "I *knew* he wasn't tall. I *knew* he was short. But somehow I always forgot, and then when he came to school to pick me up for a vacation or sometimes just for a long weekend, it was such a shock seeing him. He was short!" She giggled. "I know you think I'm an idiot for telling you this, but it's true. I can remember at least twice, once when I got off a train and once when I had to go to the front hall of the school to meet him, that I really thought someone had sent an impostor. My father, I knew, looked exactly the same, but he was taller, much taller. I knew it. I *knew* it!"

"Maybe he's shrinking," Rick offered, and rolled quickly out of the way, and she moved to shove him with one booted foot.

"I'm serious," she said.

Rick rolled on his back and looked up into the branches of the oak tree. The leaves had budded, and from here the whole sky above looked filmed with the palest green. "When I was a kid," he said, "I thought my mom was the most beautiful woman in the world. I really did. I couldn't imagine anyone ever being that beautiful." He looked at Neal. She was lying with one elbow propping up her head. Her dark hair had fallen forward, hiding half her face.

"What happened?" she asked.

Rick sighed. "We went away for a vacation somewhere—my grandmother's or somewhere—and when I came back, I had a new teacher. Her name was Miss Wright, and one look at her and I thought, Wow!" He laughed. "And that was it for mom, I guess."

"You beast!" Neal said. "You mean you took one look at your new teacher and dumped your mom."

"HmmmHmm." Rick nodded. He snapped his fingers. "Like that. One minute, mom was Miss Universe, and the next"—another snap of his fingers—"she was just mom."

"Well," Neal said, "I can see you're a good man to stay away from. You could never be sure when another Miss Wright might be around the corner." She gazed down the slope to where they had tethered the horses. The gray stallion was standing proud, looking out over the rolling countryside, while the mare munched on grass.

"What was she like?" Neal asked.

"Who?" Rick asked innocently. He knew she meant Miss Wright.

"I'm warning you," Neal said.

"Ordinary," he said. He watched the stallion nuzzle the mare's neck as she grazed. "She got married and moved away, and I thought that my heart would break. She came to school one day and showed us this big ring on her finger with a diamond and all, and she sat us down and explained all about marriage and love and everything and that she was going to get married and have her own family, and I thought my heart would break. I saw the guy she was going to marry. He came to school to pick her up one day, and I hated him." Rick laughed. "I mean, I *really* hated him. Then, about two or three years later, in a shopping center in D.C., I ran into them Christmas shopping with their own little baby in a stroller, and you know what? Miss Wright was just like everybody else to me."

"Ordinary," Neal said.

"Yeah," Rick admitted. "Special ordinary, but ordinary."

"Like daddy," Neal said.

Rick found it hard to think of Uncle Toots as ordinary under any circumstances.

"I mean," Neal said, "in my mind, the biggest, most powerful man in the world, and then I would see him and he was . . ."

She wouldn't say "ordinary," and Rick liked her for that. He helped her. "Like everybody else," he suggested.

"Yes," she said. "But I just wish he would understand that I'm like everybody else, too."

Rick nearly said, "But you're not." The afternoon heat had made him drowzy, and the nearness of Neal made his senses float in a mixture of excitement and confusion. He wanted to reach out and touch her arm, put his arms around her and draw her close to him, and while he let his mind float away on that daydream, the stallion neighed angrily nearby, and Rick was jolted back to the present, not entirely sure that his hands had not, of themselves, reached toward this girl for whom he had such strong feelings.

She was looking away from him so that he saw her face in profile, the straight line of her nose, the full mouth, the clear forehead and the wide eyes staring off across the land, bursting forth with the renewed energy of a new spring. "Do you suppose it's always like that?" she asked.

"How?" But he thought he knew.

"Do you suppose that all the people you love are really very ordinary, that one day you would wake up and see them differently?"

"No," Rick said.

He said nothing else, and when he didn't, she turned to face him. "Why are you so sure?" she asked.

He could have answered, "Because I think I'm in love with you." But one last strand of common sense kept him silent.

"You don't know, do you?" she asked. It was a challenge.

"Maybe love is a spell," he suggested. That

was the way he had been feeling lately, as
though he had been put under a spell. He had
almost reached out and tried to take her in his
arms, and he had one clear, terrible thought of
how she would have reacted to that. He could
feel the blood rise to his face at the mere
thought of the embarrassment if he had done
that. "You fall under the spell of someone else,
and if you're very lucky, they fall under your
spell."

She was smiling. "And if you're *really* lucky,"
she said, "you both stay under the same spell
forever."

They held each other's glances, she staring
down into his eyes from where she lay propped
up on her elbow and he, on his back, looking up
at her face, framed by the halo of pale oak
leaves lit by the last rays of the afternoon sun.

Her face seemed to float just above his, and
Rick seemed to lose some moments in time. His
heart raced, and he felt he was on the brink of a
new world; then loudly, stridently, the stallion
neighed, and they both blinked, Neal and Rick,
as though awakening from their own spells.
They were in the countryside again, with the
sun setting quickly behind the horizon, casting
the first shadows of evening across the land.

Neal shivered and pulled her jacket about
her. She stood up fast, and they remounted
their horses. They rode back silently through

the quickening twilight, and as they came to the last rise before the lane down to the stable, she turned to Rick and said, "I'll say one thing, Rick Prescott. You're not ordinary." Then she spurred her horse and rode off fast toward home.

7

Rick awakened to the sound of a heavy spring rain pounding on the roof. Lazily, he reached up and drew back the curtain on the window beside the bed. Outside, the world was gray and wet.

Sunday, his half-awake mind counseled him. He had homework assignments to prepare, his clothes to wash, chores to do around the house for Harley and Adele. He slipped back into a warm, content sleep and dreamed of palm trees and oranges that grew on trees outside the kitchen window and a girl with gold-flecked eyes who rode haughtily along a pink beach.

"Hey, loverboy," Adele's voice broke into his dream. "Breakfast."

Rick sat up in bed. Adele's head, adorned with bright-green plastic curlers, was speaking to him from his doorway.

"Twenty minutes, no fuss, come as you are," the head told him with a smile before it disappeared and the door shut.

Rick blinked. The sight of Adele in curlers before he was fully awake, while he was still dreaming of pink beaches and long-haired girls, had given him a rude shock. Now he stretched and yawned. The long week and the ride of yesterday had dropped him into ten long, much-needed hours of sleep.

He felt wonderful. He felt he could take on the whole world. He lay for a few more minutes listening to the rain, imagining the hills where he had cantered yesterday with Neal in sunshine, now swept with sheets of rain to nourish the young growth. Did they have seasons in Florida? What would it be like to have sunshine every day? Would every day be the same? He loved the change of seasons, spring rains, the hot, humid summer, and the autumn that burst like fire over the country and then cooled into winter again.

The smell of bacon drew him out of bed more surely than a fire bell. He took his blue robe from the door, wrapped himself in it and plodded down the hall to the bathroom. He didn't know what he had expected, but he looked exactly as he had for a while with small variations: tall, curly-haired, blond, a boy turning into a man. But he felt different. He felt as if something important had happened to him, and that should show.

"I'm in love," he told his reflection. He was sure of it. The sight of Neal cantering off down the lane, shadowed by the first minutes of night, came back to him and with it his feeling as though some force had squeezed on his heart and the other feelings—a wish to hold her, to tell her everything that he had ever thought, everything that had ever happened to him, and to hear the same from her so they could be closer than they'd ever been, either of them, to anyone else.

"You're not ordinary, Rick Prescott." What had she meant by that?

"Where is that bum Rick Prescott?" Harley's voice shouted down the hall, breaking up Rick's reveries of the day before and its ending.

"Coming, coming," Rick shouted, following the rich, mixed odors of toast and coffee, bacon and waffles.

Adele, crowned with her bright-green curlers, was sitting at the kitchen table while Harley dished up waffles from the old waffle iron set on the center of the stove. "Rick Prescott, bum, reporting for duty," Rick said as he walked into the kitchen.

After breakfast, Adele went into her room and closed the door. She spent Sundays in bed reading romances. Harley got very quiet, the way he did when he was thinking, and soon Rick saw him bent over his desk working on an elaborate graph. Rick did his own laundry in the basement, changed the sheets on his bed and sat down to try to catch up on his homework, but his mind wasn't on it. He would work for a few minutes on his English composition, then catch himself looking out the window at the rain washing down the glass, and beyond that the budding apple trees of the back yard.

Finally, he admitted to himself what was wrong. He couldn't get Neal out of his mind. He went back to the kitchen and quietly shut the door. The phone on the wall looked as frightening as a rattlesnake near her nest. He reached twice for it and stopped before he finally picked it up, and even then he listened to the dial tone until it shrieked angrily, as though the receiver were off the hook. He hung the receiver up again, took a deep breath and shoved his hands deep into the pockets of his worn, Sunday jeans.

"Prescott, you idiot," he murmured to himself. "She doesn't want to hear from you."

He imagined her up there on Linden Hill, the rain coming down beyond those long windows of the living room and a fire roaring, Toots hanging about and Neal maybe reading a book or a magazine. Then he imagined the phone ringing and a maid answering. He went cold at the thought of a maid going into that living room with Toots and Neal in front of the fire and saying Rick Prescott was calling.

Back in his room, he worked some more on the English composition, but nothing he wrote made any sense. He went back to the kitchen and dialed Neal's number.

He heard the phone ringing at the end of the line, and he tried to picture where it would be in the house on Linden Hill. They probably had a dozen phones all over the house.

"Shaw residence," a voice said.

Rick's throat had gone dry. "Is Neal there?" he managed to croak out.

"Can I tell her who's calling?" the voice asked. That was the maid, Rick realized.

"Rick," he said.

A small silence. "Just Rick?" the voice asked.

Rick knew he was meant to give his whole name then, but somehow the tone of the maid's voice got him mad. "Yeah," he said. "Just Rick."

He heard the maid put the phone down on a hard surface; then he heard a lot of other sounds far off—voices, the sound of a door shutting, then footsteps. Neal said, "Hi, Just Rick." She was laughing.

"Is that what she said?" he asked.

"That's what she said. There's a Just Rick on the phone."

"Well," Rick admitted after a second or two, "it's true. I'm a 'Just Rick,' nothing else."

Neal laughed. "Sounds good to me," she said. "What are you up to, 'Just Rick.'"

Rick took a chance. "I was thinking of you," he admitted. Then he added hastily, "Thought maybe you'd like to talk to a friend."

Neal said, "How brave are you feeling?"

"Why?"

"You want to come up here for dinner again? I was just sitting around reading. I could come get you."

The thought of going through another dinner at Linden Hill chilled Rick as cold as the spring rain outside. "Will Toots be there?" he asked weakly.

"He lives here," Neal pointed out.

"You drive a hard bargain," Rick said.

"I'm not Toots Shaw's daughter for nothing," Neal said. "You want me to come get you?"

"Okay," Rick agreed.

Once he had hung up, Rick felt a surge of happiness go through him. He wanted to pick up the telephone and call Florida and tell his mom he was going to spend the afternoon with the most wonderful girl he had ever met; he wanted to run through the house and shout to Adele and Harley; he wanted to tell someone, but he realized that there really wasn't anyone he could tell without looking like an idiot. He was invited up to Linden Hill to spend the rest of the afternoon with Neal and then have dinner. *Correction:* he had invited himself up to Linden Hill to spend the rest of the afternoon and have dinner. With a friend. That was it. He went on back to his bedroom, past the living room, and thought it was just as well he hadn't run shouting through the house about his plans. Adele was asleep in the living room with a paperback romance in her lap, and Harley was bent over his desk in his bedroom.

"I'm going out for dinner," Rick said from the door.

Harley looked up, nodded distractedly, and went back to his work.

In his bedroom, Rick went through the old routine of trying to find something to wear. He knew girls did that, but he wondered if they knew boys did it as much as girls did. But search as he did, he couldn't find anything except his favorite old beige cords and a flannel shirt faded from red to rose. "Just Rick," he told his mirror as he smoothed the wrinkles out of the front of the shirt. He tried to see how he would look to Neal. His blond hair needed cutting, he saw, and he was growing fast; the shirt stretched across his chest, open at the neck to show his white T-shirt. Nothing fancy, he thought. Just Rick.

He took his rain jacket and went out to wait for Neal. The rain swept in curtains across the road, and the apple boughs dripped water into sodden grass. His mom and Kenny were probably lying in the sun on some beach with the kids, Rick thought, but to him, the sight of the red sports car throwing off a wave of water as it came down the lane was a better sight than any beach or warm blue water.

"You look great," he told Neal when he got in the car. She did. She was wearing jeans and an old white crew-neck sweater. Her hair was pulled back from her face with a white ribbon tied at the neck. She looked . . . friendly, he decided.

"I'm glad you called," she admitted as she gunned the car away from the house. "I didn't want to call you. I was afraid you'd think I was too forward."

Rick couldn't bring himself to believe that anything could scare Neal Shaw, but he knew he didn't really know her. He just knew what he had seen from the outside, and he knew that a lot of the time what people saw of *him* didn't give the right picture. Sometimes he thought he was two people. The outside person and the inside person. "I was scared half to death to call you," he said.

She looked at him, surprised. "Me?" she said.

"You're sort of . . ." He couldn't find the word.

Still, she protested. "I am not," she said. She

took the corner faster than Rick thought safe for the road.

"If you don't mind," he joked when they were all the way around the corner, "I'd sort of like to live to graduate. Just curious, you know. Want to see if there's life after high school."

Neal slowed down. She drove more sedately for the next few moments, sneaking little side looks at Rick. He could see her doing it without facing her, and he knew he sometimes did that, too, with people. The more he got to know Neal Shaw, the more it was like seeing another side of himself. That thought sort of shook him up for a couple of seconds. If she was really like him, that opened up all sorts of other doors through which his thoughts could wander.

As they turned in at the gates of Linden Hill, Neal said, "I expect I'll be a better driver when I've had more practice."

All other thoughts fled. "How long have you had your license?" he asked.

Neal looked at him. "About three months," she told him seriously.

Rick placed his hands as carefully as he could on the dashboard without looking too panicked as she crushed the edge of a flower bed and came to a stop. He swallowed hard, but said nothing.

Still, she seemed to feel a rebuke. "You don't have much use for a driver's license in a boarding school," she said with a return of her old asperity. "Everyone has to learn sometime."

That was true, Rick agreed, following her into the house. He wondered if the driving instructor still taught driving or had chosen another profession, such as going into a monastery to meditate, since his bout with Neal behind the wheel.

The inside of Linden Hill smelled like no house Rick had ever been in. He tried to figure it out as he followed Neal down the hall, and when it hit him, he nearly laughed out loud. The inside of Linden Hill smelled like a really clean hotel—furniture polish, lemon oil, no dust, clean sheets and drapes. But the room into which Neal took him was quite different. This was a small yellow room with two huge chairs in a flower-covered cloth by a small fire of pine logs. There was a yellow carpet on the floor and a white and yellow patterned bamboo wallpaper. Two French windows hung with long sheer curtains gave off onto a small walled garden. "This was my mother's room," Neal said.

This room smelled of the fire and a faint, faraway reminder of Neal's own perfume. Rick wanted to sink down on the carpet in front of the fire, kick off his loafers, and never leave.

As though reading his mind, Neal kicked off her own shoes and curled up in one of the big chairs. "Almost all my memories of my childhood take place in this room," Neal said, looking about. There was a picture of a man and a very pretty woman who looked like Neal. Rick stared at it and realized finally that the man standing beside the woman was Toots, but a different Toots. The man in the picture was grinning from ear to ear as though someone had just made him emperor of the world and he was as surprised as anybody else but would do his best, anyway. The Toots Rick had seen walking in and out of the garage all week had a scowl on his face, as though his indigestion were acting up again. "Daddy and my mother used to spend a lot of time in here. She loved this room. Daddy liked having the big house, but my mother really only needed this room. We haven't—" she searched around for a way to say it—"lived like this very long," she said. "It means a lot to Toots, but my mother didn't really care about it."

Rick put the picture back. "He looks really happy," he said.

"Yes," Neal admitted. "They loved each other a lot. I can remember that clearly."

Rick sat down in the other chair. He liked the quiet of this huge house. He was used to the small house where he had lived with Kenny and his mom and the kids. Noise exploded through that house; happy noise, it was true, but noise. This house here seemed to ooze peace. Rick began to think about Toots in a different way.

Neal was staring at Rick.

"What are you thinking?" he asked.

"That was always daddy's chair," Neal said.

Rick had a creeping feeling that Toots was still there sitting in it. He thought it would be too rude to get up right after she had said that, but that was what he wanted to do.

Now another worry rose in his mind. He began to feel uncomfortable for a second because he couldn't think of anything to say and the silence was getting too long. He just wanted to look at her and look at her.

Finally, Neal broke the silence. "Do you like old movies?" she asked.

Truth was, he didn't know. He almost never watched old movies. "Sure," he said.

"There's a great one on," Neal said, opening a small cabinet and revealing a television set. "I was going to watch it before you called." She switched it on and went back to the chair. Rick took the chance to slide onto the floor, which was where he had wanted to sit, anyway, but he wanted to sit there even more since he knew he was sitting in Toots' chair. The movie was about a long sea voyage and a man and a woman who didn't like each other at first, then did, then didn't, then finally gave up and decided they loved each other.

The time passed, and Rick found that he was again more comfortable than he had ever been, and he wanted this afternoon to go on forever.

At one point, without thinking, he turned, and using the poker, moved the logs on the fire, then threw another on. It wasn't until he had finished that he thought maybe he was being rude. He had done it automatically, the way he would at home or at Adele's and Harley's. But Neal was watching him with a nice small smile as though she appreciated that he had done it, and he settled back on the floor at her feet to watch the end of the movie.

The movie had just ended, and Neal was closing the doors to the cabinet when a familiar voice was heard calling, "Neal, you there?" Toots was coming down the hall.

Rick's heart raced with apprehension. He had a pretty good idea that Toots wouldn't be thrilled to see him. The look on Toots' face when he opened the door and stepped into the yellow room more or less confirmed it. He was looking really pleased; then, at the sight of Rick, he looked as though, without warning, he had come upon a freeway accident.

"Rick came over to watch television and have dinner," Neal said.

Toots looked at the other yellow chair, and Rick had a sense of relief that he wasn't sitting in it when Toots came in. "Thought I'd come spend a minute with you before dinner," he said moodily.

He came into the room, and Rick felt out of place, as though there wasn't room for all three of them there at the same time. Toots seemed to feel something of the same thing. He opened the French doors. A gust of cold, damp air took the warmth from the room. "Brad called," Toots said.

Neal didn't reply. She busied herself with tidying up the books on the table near her chair. "Sit down, daddy," she said. "Relax; dinner won't be for another half hour."

"I have some work to do," he said. But before he left, he nodded in halfhearted cordiality to Rick.

If there had been some way to get out of dinner, Rick would have done it. He was thinking of excuses when Neal said, "Don't worry, Rick." He looked at her. She wasn't laughing at him or even smiling. She was almost pleading, not quite, but she was really worried herself, and he knew once again how lonely she was. "He's not really like that. He just gets . . . dumb," was the best she could come up with. "He was so poor once, and now he's not, and he worries about me. He just doesn't understand that I'm not some little girl who has to be taken care of for the rest of her life."

Rick at that moment couldn't think of anything he would like better than to take care of Neal for the rest of her life, but he let it go. "You think that happens when you become a father or mother?" he asked. "You think when you become a mother or father, you go sort of strange and forget what you were like as a teenager and think your kids are so dumb they can't look after themselves. My mom, when she went to Florida with Kenny, acted like I was a puppy she was leaving out overnight or something."

Neal laughed. "That's Toots," she agreed. "On the one hand, he thinks I'm the greatest girl since I don't know when; on the other, he thinks I'm so helpless that if he doesn't set me up with . . . well, with everything he thinks a girl needs—money and houses and all that— then I'll end up destitute or something."

They were close again. Toots and his ill humor had drifted away. They talked about little things then—movies, Linden, the rain, nothing special and everything special because *they* were talking about it—until it was time for dinner.

This time, the three of them were all placed at one end of the table, Rick and Toots facing each other like adversaries and Neal, at the end, between them. Toots had decided to make an effort for Neal. "So," he said to Rick as the maid went out with the salad bowl. Rick had managed to get salad without dropping any. Serving yourself was like riding a bicycle, he decided; once you learned, you didn't forget. And as Neal had said about her driving, everyone had to learn. "What are you going to do when you get out of school? Go to work?"

"Go to college," Rick said. "My mom and my stepfather have moved to Florida, which is why I have to work to stay here for a while and finish school. I'm going to Florida to college, I guess."

Toots thought about that while he munched on a lettuce leaf like an angry rabbit. "When I was a boy . . ." he began.

After that, it was easy. Toots talked straight through about his own boyhood, his youth, his success, while Rick and Neal threw each other little amused looks every now and then; with every look, Rick felt he was getting closer to Neal. He served himself perfectly, and after dinner even Toots seemed to find some good in Rick. Not many people, Rick reflected, probably listened to him talk straight through a whole meal without wanting to say a word themselves, but Rick was just happy to be there with Neal. Toots could talk all he liked.

When they got up from the table, Rick said, "I hate to eat and run, but I still have homework to do. I'm afraid I have to go."

"I'll drive you back," Neal said.

Toots went so far as to shake Rick's hand. But he did add to Neal, "Be back soon. Gets dark and dangerous. Never know who's out there."

Neal and Rick went out into the night. The rain had stopped. The night smelled of wet, fallow earth. Pale clouds drifted before the stars. They drove home in a silence that for Rick was part contentment, part excitement. When Neal pulled up in front of Adele's house, she said, "Thank you, Rick, for calling."

He couldn't think of anything to say.

"See you," was the best he could come up with. Then quickly, he added, "Soon."

"Okay," Neal said.

Rick watched her drive away. He didn't think he had ever been as happy in his life.

8

You've got troubles, friend," Harley said as Rick came up the walk to the school.

Rick felt as though he were walking on a cloud. "No troubles, buddy," he said, slapping Harley on the shoulder. "No troubles I can't handle."

"I wouldn't be too sure of that," Harley said, gesturing with a nod toward the student parking lot. Brad Rawson stood leaning against the black Charger, his arms crossed, glowering in Rick's direction. His buddies stood about him as though it were their girls Rick had run off with instead of Brad's. "The pack's not happy," Harley said. "The Pack" was Harley's expression for the group of guys who had their own cars and plenty of money in their pockets, who walked around as though they owned the school.

Rick had never had many friends. Living out in the country without a car of his own, he hadn't been able to get around much, date much, hang out. He had tried out for the teams, and had played both basketball and football, but he also had always had to have a part-time job, so he couldn't make as many practices as the other guys, and finally he'd been dropped. He went to all the school dances, and he was popular, but he'd never had a steady girl.

I've never had a girl friend, he was thinking as he walked on up the steps and into the school. And I've never had a girl who was a friend. He thought about Neal as he stored his books into his locker and got ready for his first class, English. "What I need is a friend," she had said across the table in the diner. Even conjured up in his mind's eye, she was the most beautiful girl he had ever seen, and she said she wanted him for her friend. He felt in some strange way as though his life, his real life, had begun and everything that had happened had led up to his meeting Neal.

"Hey, pretty boy," Brad Rawson said behind him. "How does it feel to have a girl drive you around?"

Rick took a deep breath, more a sigh. With his thick, blond curls he'd had a lot of kidding in his life. When he was a baby, women used to stop his mother on the street and say what a beautiful little girl she had, and his young stepsister was forever moaning about her long straight hair that wouldn't take a curl. He'd been teased since elementary school when one of the boys said he should play softball instead of baseball and he'd rubbed the kid's face in the grass until he changed his tune.

He turned slowly to face Brad Rawson. Rawson stood a half-dozen feet away, his heavy brows knit, eyes slight with mischief, cohorts spread out on either side. Rick thought of a half-dozen replies from "Get Lost" to "Grow up" before he found the one he wanted. He smiled slowly and said, "Feels good, Rawson. Feels good," and he walked right at the Pack as they stood ranged in a half circle before him. Just before they parted to let him through, he had the satisfaction of seeing the blood rise in a furious flush up the thick stem of Brad Rawson's neck; then he was through them and walking down the hall toward class.

"Hey, Prescott," Rawson shouted as Rick kept up a steady, unhurried pace toward the classroom, his heart beating faster than usual, ready at any minute for more trouble. But whatever Rawson was going to shout after Rick to save his own face was lost in the ringing of the school bell that exploded through the halls, drowning out all other sound.

"If you're planning to commit hari-kari,"

Harley said, slipping into the seat beside Rick, "you might let me know so Adele can rent out your room."

"I don't intend to do anything except go to school, go to work, and be friendly," Rick told him with the same slow smile, except warmer. "I don't have time for anything else."

Brad Rawson and his friends came into class, followed by Miss Smith, the sturdy, overweight English teacher who had taught at Linden High for twenty-five years. She was known as the "Tank," and even Brad Rawson wasn't up to making trouble with the "Tank" in command, so soon the class was lost in the complexities of poetry. Rick listened with half an ear while thinking back to his afternoon with Neal—the way her eyes sparkled when she spoke, how her hair fell across her brow when she leaned forward to listen to something he was saying, the texture of her skin, like a frosted rose petal.

The morning classes passed half in a dream. He saw Harley watching him as he moved from room to room—science, algebra, physics—and at lunch hour, Harley came over and said, "Room for more than one in that dream?"

Rick and Harley nearly always lunched together. They had since they were kids. "That obvious, huh?" Rick said.

"Well, either you're drugged, or you're in love," Harley said.

"I am drugged with love," Rick said. He felt

bigger, all grown up suddenly, and he wanted to tell Harley about it. They went out through the side door of the school. They walked to the running track and climbed up through the stands until they could sit with their backs against the panel at the top and eat their lunches in the sun. From there they had a view of the whole school layout—the main building of plain red brick, the parking lot where the student and faculty cars were left each day, the football field, and the baseball diamond. A junior high school track team came out of the locker rooms with their coach and started to limber up. The juniors, who, Rick had to remind himself, were only one year younger than he, seemed like little children to him. He watched how seriously they took their practice, making work of play, and could remember how important all that had seemed to him. He was a good athlete and had a natural body that responded to the challenges he set for it. One of the hardest moments this year had been when he realized he couldn't try out for any teams because he wouldn't have time to work, to go to school, and to play competitively.

But you had to set your priorities. He knew that, and an education was more important to him right now than anything else in his life. An education would pay off for the rest of his life.

Harley, whose idea of sports was to open the door of his old car and put himself behind the

wheel, wouldn't have understood, so Rick
didn't dwell on it.

"She sure is a beautiful girl," Harley said for
openers.

Rick munched on his sandwich. He wanted to
talk about Neal, and he didn't. He wanted to
tell everyone that they had spent the afternoon
together, that they were friends, and yet that
friendship was the most special thing in the
world to him right now, and he didn't want to
share it. He wanted to keep it to himself, as
though if he talked about it, it would go away,
and he would lose it.

He wasn't good with words the way Harley
was. What he said was "She's nice, too."

Now Harley said nothing for a while. That
wasn't unusual. Like many good friends, Harley
and Rick knew how to be quiet together, enjoy-
ing each other's company; sometimes, when
one or the other spoke after a long silence, they
would find that they had been thinking the same
things.

Rick watched the juniors line up under the
coach's direction. There were three boys and a
girl. Times were changing. A couple of years
ago, there would have only been boys. The girls
had their own track team, too, but if a girl
wanted to compete against a boy, she could just
up and say so. This girl down on the track was a
serious athlete. The way she limbered up her
legs, stretching them one at a time, bending her

body and arching her back, showed how serious she was. Her concentration was intense.

"What's it like up there on the hill?" Harley asked.

Rick had been thinking about Neal as he watched the girl, about her life on Linden Hill and how Toots had kept her away from this small town all that time, kept her wrapped up and stashed away like something very fragile, a Christmas ornament, maybe, to be brought out once a year to be placed on the top of the tree.

"Rich," Rick said.

Harley laughed. "Yeah, I bet. Gold bathroom fixtures, huh?"

"Never went into the john," Rick said, "but I wouldn't be surprised. Toots would like that." Then, as the juniors got into starting position for a practice race, he added, "Neal's not like that."

The coach dropped his arm and shouted as though a gun had gone off, and the juniors shot out of their starting positions. The girl dropped back to the middle of the pack, holding her pace steadily, and Rick liked what he was seeing. He'd done enough running himself to know that she was saving her strength. The front runner, a cocky little kid with curly black hair, was strutting away in the front of the pack like a winner, but Rick knew that he wouldn't win. He'd set the pace, and then one of the other runners who had been holding back in the pack would put on that last spurt and take the victory away from him.

A shout of laughter from the distance drew their attention. Over in the parking lot, a group of boys was gathered around the black Charger that belonged to Brad Rawson. Half a dozen girls stood a few feet away.

"You think guys like us ever get the girl?" Harley asked.

Rick faced him. Harley was his friend, but he didn't think of himself as being just like Harley. Still, he knew what Harley meant. "Why not?" he asked, and as he did so, he knew he didn't want this conversation to go on much longer. Harley had a way of saying the obvious, the thing that you knew but didn't want to face.

"I don't know," Harley said. "Some people just sort of belong together, you know, and others don't." Rick knew Harley didn't mean to be cruel. Harley liked the truth. He was going to be a scientist, and he liked to look at the evidence and follow that wherever the trail led. What Harley was saying in his own way was that Rick came from a different background than Neal. Brad Rawson, with all that family money behind him, would understand her better. Brad Rawson wouldn't knock over the platter at dinner.

The runners were coming around for their

final lap. Rick made a point of leaning forward as though absorbed in the race. Harley knew Rick well enough not to pursue the conversation. The short, fast-paced kid who had led the pack had dropped back, run-out before the course was over. The race was now between the girl and a tall, skinny boy with legs like a bird that pumped up and down, up and down. The girl wasn't giving up. She pushed him all the way to the line, losing by a fraction of a second.

She had guts, that girl, Rick thought. What about Neal? What did she have? She had a father who loved her, and she'd been given everything she ever wanted. She would expect to be taken care of all her life. Rick thought of his mom and her struggles to make ends meet over the bad months. She and Kenny had pulled together.

When he actually got down to it, he had to admit to himself that he really knew almost nothing about Neal Shaw. Why, then, did he feel so strongly about her? He'd never felt this way about anyone before.

The loud ringing of the school bell brought him back to the present. He didn't know Neal, he had to remind himself as he followed Harley down the steps to the track, and she didn't know him.

The red sports car was waiting when he came out of the school building at the end of the day.

Harley saw it first. "I guess you're taken care of," he said. Usually, Harley gave Rick a ride to work. Rick saw the car then. Neal had the top up, but he could recognize her profile even if that hadn't been the only car of its type in Linden.

He found he was blushing.

Brad Rawson and his crowd had come out of the school building. Brad took one look at the car, scowled, and started off toward the car lot. Then he changed his mind, spun on his heel and started toward the red car. Rick wasn't sure what to do. On the one hand, he knew, as though it were planned, that Neal was here to see him, but on the other, they were just friends, and he could make a fool of himself if he interfered.

Still, better to make a fool of himself, he decided fast, than to be thought of as a guy who could be driven away by a jerk like Brad. So, taking a deep breath, he, too, started toward the car.

He knew as he took the steps one by one that everyone was watching. Brad Rawson reached the car while Rick was only halfway there. From where Rick was, he could hear Brad as he leaned down into the driver's window and said, "Hello there, stranger." The way he said it, he made it into a little bit of a joke, as though he were mocking Neal, and that made Rick mad.

He knew why Brad was doing it and why he was talking loud enough for everyone to hear. Brad wanted them all to think he thought all this was a joke, that he had lost nothing in his argument with Neal and that her friendship with Rick itself was a joke.

Neal turned away, looking toward Rick as he approached.

Rick took a deep breath. The truth was he felt helpless. He wasn't afraid of Brad, and if it came to a fight, he knew he could match Brad, but that wasn't Rick's style at all. He was being taunted into an argument by Brad Rawson, an argument he couldn't win. If he fought back, he was as bad as Brad; if he didn't, he would look as if he were scared.

Not getting an answer, Brad leaned on the convertible top to watch Rick approach. Brad had the same small, mocking smile he'd had this morning. Rick's heart had started to beat faster than usual, but whatever happened, he was determined not to make the first move.

Neal solved the moment. Inside the car, she pressed the button to lower the top, and suddenly the roof rose, startling Brad and making him step back. Rick opened the passenger door of the car, slid in, and they were off, out of the parking lot before the first wave of laughter had broken over the furious Brad Rawson.

"Making lots of friends," Rick commented.

"Was he your friend before?" Neal asked.

"No, but he wasn't my enemy, either," Rick said. Still, he started to laugh suddenly at the sight of Brad's leaping back from the roof as it rose and slid into the rear compartment of the car. "You are a wicked lady," he said.

He was rewarded with a swift, mischievous smile. "Did I embarrass you coming to school?" she asked.

"Yes," he admitted.

"Would you prefer I hadn't come?"

"No," he confessed.

She drove sedately along the back roads, anticipating the corners as though she had lived there all her life. Rick said so. "Well, I did for a long time," she pointed out to him. "And when I was away at school, sometimes when I was going to sleep in the dormitory, I would try to imagine what it was like back here so I wouldn't forget." She looked at him sideways. "It's strange not to have a home town, you know. People ask where you're from, and I was from Linden, but if I didn't really stop and try to remember what Linden was like, I would find it was fading away from me. So I made a game of it, picturing different streets and roads as I remembered them, and when I came back, the few times when Toots didn't take me somewhere else for my vacations, I would check out my memory."

Rick knew she called her father "daddy" to his face. But away from him she called him "Toots," like the rest of the town. Toots was sort of like a local monument or hero; he was just "Toots." Even Neal found it hard to describe "Toots" as "daddy" when she wasn't actually talking to him.

The thought of Toots brought up another thought. "I have to be at work soon," Rick said regretfully.

"Okay," Neal said. Then, a few minutes later, she said, "You know, I really don't go around picking up strange boys." She checked to see if he believed her. "I mean," she said, "I know almost nothing about boys. I've been in a girls' school for years and years." She laughed. "I'm practically a nun. That's what happened with Brad, if you're wondering. I mean he asked me to go over to his house to watch television, and when I got there, I thought it kind of strange that there was no one there but him. I mean no servants or anything . . ."

"That sometimes happens at our house, too," Rick joked gently. "You get there, and there are no servants."

"I'm being serious," Neal said.

"So am I," Rick told her.

"You know what I mean," she admonished him.

He did, but still he had a sneaking moment of

sympathy for old Brad there, too. Neal Shaw lived in a stranger world than even Rick had thought, stranger than even Brad knew.

"Anyway," she said, and now her mouth began to twitch with the same mischievous smile, "we were watching television in the den, and he slid over the couch and . . ."

The car had reached a bend in the road that led onto the highway. She bit her lip and concentrated on the stop and the turn onto the highway. They had driven another hundred yards before Rick could hold back no longer. "And what?" he demanded. It was somehow very important to him.

"And he put his arm around my shoulder," she said.

Rick waited.

Nothing.

"So?" he asked.

"So?" she said, looking at him outraged. "I hardly know the guy. I mean daddy is trying to set something up, but I don't know him at all, and he's been over for dinner, but that's it. Then suddenly POW! THE ARM!"

Rick started to laugh. He couldn't help himself. "That was it?" he asked.

"Well, how was I to know what came next?" she said.

"Poor Brad," Rick said.

Neal Shaw got a stubborn look, not unlike

the look her father got when a customer came back and demanded service under warranty. But it passed. "Anyway, I belted out of there fast, and he followed, and I got scared," she said more quietly, "and just kept driving faster and faster until I saw you."

"Who you tried to run down," Rick said.

Up ahead, the revolving sign UNCLE TOOTS' CARNIVAL OF CARS was a tiny speck against the blue of the afternoon sky. Rick wished he didn't have to go to work. He wished he could float along in this expensive car with Neal beside him and talk and talk and talk. He wanted to know so much more about Neal; he wanted to know everything about Neal. Sometimes he felt as though he had known her all his life, and sometimes he felt she was the strangest person he had ever met.

He sneaked a look at her sideways. She was so beautiful to him that he found it hard to believe he was here with her. His life had been going along one way, and then POW! She'd come racing down the road, and now he had a whole lot of other feelings he wasn't sure about.

The sign seemed to remind Neal of something, too. She slowed the car. She wanted to say something. He knew it, but she couldn't find any way to say it, either. What she did say finally, just as the car dealership was looming up, was "I feel like a stranger in Linden."

"You don't have to," he said as she slowed to a complete stop by the dealership.

She looked at him. "I don't want to," she said. "I want to belong. That's why I came home, not because of any of Toots' ideas. Will you help me?"

"Sure," Rick said slowly. "I'll help you."

Then there was a silence, not uncomfortable but long enough that they both knew the other wanted to say something and couldn't find the right words. Rick put his hand on the door handle. "Work calls," he said reluctantly. He got out.

"I'll hold you to your word," Neal said, smiling.

"Promise?" he asked her.

"Promise," she said. Then she saw something behind him, and her expression changed slightly, and she said coolly, "Good-bye, Rick."

The car pulled away, and Rick felt a confusion at the sudden change of signals he had felt from Neal until he turned to walk up to the dealership. There, outside the showroom, was Toots Shaw. He didn't look any too happy at the sight of his daughter dropping Rick off.

As Rick walked up past him, Toots said, "You're late."

Rick looked through the plate-glass window at the showroom clock. "Two minutes," he said.

"That's still late," Toots replied, and turning on his heel, walked off in the other direction.

9

The sun appeared as a halo behind Neal's hair as the boat drifted slowly downstream on the current. Rick lay back, his arms folded behind his head.

"What are you smiling at?" Neal asked him. She sat on the cross-board of the old rowboat that Rick and Harley had found years ago and kept hidden down the river for days just like this, unusually warm for this early in the year.

"Was I smiling?" he asked innocently. Truly, he hadn't known he was smiling. He smiled a lot these days. Harley had commented on it.

"Like a cat," Neal said.

The current took the boat and spun it gently in a circle so that the sun moved away from behind her. The willows on the banks trailed long, thin branches in the water. "I guess I'm happy," he told her.

The sun now fell full on her face. Neal was happy, too, he thought. But her moods shifted so fast he sometimes thought he didn't know her at all. "What was your father like?" she asked suddenly.

He took his time before he answered her. He'd thought about his father a lot in the years when he was growing up. At first, he had hoped and hoped that his mom would remarry his father. Later, after she met Kenny and married him and he had known she was happy with him, he had deliberately kept his father separate in his head from Kenny and his mom.

"I haven't seen him in a long time," he said.

She let a few seconds go by. "That wasn't what I asked," she said.

He didn't want to talk about his father. He never talked about him. Once in a while, his mom and he, if they were alone, might say something that brought his father up, but mostly they were careful not to talk about him. His mom had loved his dad—he was sure of that— but they hadn't been able to live together, and she was never really able to explain why, not to Rick and, Rick was sure, not to herself.

"He was a kid," he said finally.

Neal laughed, not a laugh of amusement, but more one of surprise.

"I'm serious," Rick said. He sat up in the

boat to check where they were. He knew the river as well as he had known his old room at home. He could lie flat on his back, and by checking the horizon, know where he was, but in the spring the runoff from the rains could make the current treacherous.

They were about halfway downriver from the place where Harley and Rick kept the boat hidden. They kept the boat as far up the river as they could in an abandoned boathouse near the Linden Hill estate that Toots now owned. The people who owned the land where the boathouse was seldom came to Linden. The house had burned down twenty years before, and they lived in Philadelphia and just kept the land as an investment. The boathouse was the only structure left there, and that wouldn't be there long. The winter snows had caved in the roof this year, and the pilings into the river were flaking with rot.

"He was like a kid," Rick said more carefully. Sitting up in the small boat, he could smell the faint, fresh perfume of Neal's hair, which always looked beautifully clean. "He and my mom were real young when they got married, and I guess she grew up when I was born and dad didn't."

Neal sighed. "Love is so complicated, isn't it?"

Rick was pretty sure he was in love with Neal. He liked being with her more than he had ever liked being with anyone in his life. When he was apart from her, he missed her all the time. He would be doing something—his homework, working on a car, sitting in class, concentrating on what he was doing—and a feeling would come over him that was both the best and worst feeling he'd ever had. It was the worst because he would suddenly feel he'd forgotten something, something important, and then it was the best because he would remember what it was; he was missing Neal.

But he didn't think love was complicated. Love right now seemed real simple to Rick Prescott. Love hit you like lightning when you weren't expecting it, and when it did, you knew you'd been hit. "I think maybe people *make* love complicated," he said carefully.

Neal frowned. "Toots loves me," she said.

"That's different," Rick told her.

Neal stared at him for a long time. She looked right into his eyes as though searching there for something, some movement like the faint, shadowed flash of the young fish darting through the deeper pools as the boat moved downstream. She was the first girl he had ever known who didn't embarrass him when she stared at him.

"Toots wants . . ." she began.

Rick felt a flush of anger rise up into his face, and he turned away to hide it, leaning over the side of the boat to trail a hand in the ice-cold water of the river. He had a pretty good idea what Toots wanted for his daughter, and it didn't include Rick Prescott. When he was sure that the anger didn't show, he turned around again and asked, "What do *you* want?"

She knew he was serious. "I want to be happy," she said, and then, as though she had heard how spoiled that sounded, she added, "Like everybody else."

The current was taking them toward the bend in the river. Rick wished he could freeze the moment, stop the current, hold the day exactly as it was so he could first have a few moments to think. They talked about everything, and he felt more natural with her than with anyone he knew, but he kept back part of himself, too. He kept back part of himself that loved her because that wasn't what she wanted, and he was afraid that if she knew how he really felt, she'd run away from him, too.

So many people wanted something of Neal Shaw. Toots wanted her to be what he wanted her to be; Brad Rawson wanted to show her off; and even Adele and Harley, who had their own lives to live and didn't give that much thought to Neal Shaw, had an idea of how she should be—a princess, the daughter of the richest man in town. He had to be careful, Rick thought, so that Neal didn't think he, too, wanted something from her. All he wanted, Rick knew, was for Neal to be Neal. That was enough for him.

But he couldn't tell her that, and because he couldn't, there was one last, important barrier between them.

"I don't think you get happiness like a"—he looked about, searching for the word, at the banks of the river, the rolling hills, the bright blue sky and the yellow ball of the sun—"suntan," he said. And then, at that image, he changed his mind and added, "Maybe you *do* get happiness like a suntan. I mean some people spend all their time trying to be tanned, and I guess they go everywhere searching for the sun all the time, and if it rains, they get miserable and run off somewhere else. But you know, if you sit still in one place and do what you're meant to do, like take care of business, you get a tan, too, from being outside, but you also get all the other seasons, the winter, the spring, the fall. Maybe it's not meant to be summer all year long."

That was more words than he had ever put together at one time in his life when he wasn't angry. He wasn't sure that they made sense.

He knew enough about Neal, however, not to try to explain, for she was watching him again carefully, and the small smile he liked so much was playing around her lips. "Now *you're* smiling," he said.

"You're very special. You know that?" Neal said.

And now Rick did blush. Bright red. He

could feel his face redden like the bright under-wing of the robin that flew across the river right then, trailing a long, struggling worm in its beak for its young. Rick busied himself with putting the oars in the locks and then turning the boat out of the dangers of the rock shoals beneath the surface that showed, at this time of year, as a froth of white water on the surface of the river.

When he had the boat steady again, he sneaked a look at Neal. She was still watching him. "I know a lot of people who go running off looking for the sun all the time," she said.

He felt a falling away of his good feelings. Neal had a whole other life away from him that he knew nothing about. All he knew about those people was what he read in the magazines that Adele brought home from the shop. "I wouldn't know about that," he admitted. "I guess that's one way of living."

"Not many of them are happy," Neal said.

The river widened here into a small lake. The current died away, and Rick put his back into rowing the boat slowly out into the center of the lake. Along one side were picnic tables that in the summer were filled with townspeople who came down there at night after work to sit near the cool of the water. In his mind, he could see Kenny and his mom and himself down at the lake on different summer nights. Kenny would come home from work tired and hot but happy and gather them all up and take them down there. They'd cook burgers and play in the water and stay there until much later than the little kids were allowed to stay up normally. The light would die, and fireflies would spot the darkness, flaring into light and going out again just as quickly. Rick could remember many good summer nights at the lake.

Suddenly, he missed his family. He'd told himself that he was growing up and would soon be on his own, anyway, so it wasn't so bad that he'd had to stay behind for one more semester by himself, but now, floating out here on the lake with Neal beside him, he missed his mom and Kenny and the kids.

He'd been lucky, he realized like a flash of lightning across a night sky. He'd had a fine, warm family to grow up with.

He knew, just as suddenly and simply, what Neal was feeling, too. "Deep down, people are the same. Maybe different things happen to them, but people are the same."

He knew even as he said it that he was trying to convince himself as much as Neal. He wanted with every particle of his body to believe that he and Neal were the same. He didn't want to be different.

And as though she knew something of what he was feeling, she reached out then and touched him on his arm, brushing him with her finger tips as he bent forward to pull on the oars. He jumped with the shock.

The boat rocked violently, and Neal put out both hands to steady herself and make sure she wasn't thrown into the lake as Rick, recovered from his shock, dipped the oars in the water to stop the rocking. The touch of her fingers had surprised him, and now he was embarrassed to look at her. All afternoon he had wanted to reach out and touch her face gently with his own fingers, and he had known he couldn't.

When he looked at Neal, she was laughing. The laughter started as a giggle as she held tight to the sides of the boat. As he gained control, the laughter grew until, by her own movement, *she* was rocking the boat. Rick had, for one brief moment, a quick thought that she *knew* why he had reacted with such shock. Something devilish began to take over in him, and slowly but deliberately, he started to rock the boat, not so hard at first, more a challenge, then more and more. Neal's laughter slowed, tripped, hesitated, and finally she looked wary.

"Stop that, Rick Prescott," she said evenly.

"What?" he asked innocently, keeping up the rocking.

"You know what," she said, and now she was looking really worried as the dip and sway of the small boat grew.

He kept right on rocking the boat.

"Rick!" Neal cried. "We'll end up in the lake!"

"We can swim," he told her. On he rocked.

"It's cold!" she said.

"Right," he agreed. "Wake us up."

On he rocked.

Neal moved closer to him. "Don't do this, Rick," she warned him, but he could see she wasn't all that angry because her lips were twitching in a smile. Rick dipped the oars to steady the boat. He'd taught her that lesson, he thought. But before the rocking stopped, the current caught the boat, and his own heart took a leap. He'd forgotten the spring run! The boat spun around once quickly. "Rick!" Neal cried out.

Rick leaned forward, dipping the oar deep into the water, straining to pull the boat out of the current. Neal fell against him, putting both arms about his chest, holding on while he rowed steadily out of the main current, back to the center of the lake. He was sweating lightly with the effort, and he could smell the perfume of her hair more strongly now as he pulled them to safety.

The danger passed as quickly as it had struck, and they were in the center of the lake. Rick was conscious of Neal's holding onto him. He said nothing. Some seconds passed. Slowly, without looking at him, she let go. She moved farther down the boat, out of reach. Rick kept rowing steadily toward where the lake narrowed back into a stream.

Neither of them spoke of what had happened. Rick's heart hammered in his chest. He stared straight down the river at the horizon of willow trees and the sun, a darker gold as it settled toward the horizon.

A cool breeze blew across the water from the damp fields. The boat entered the mouth of the stream at the lake's end, and Rick shipped the oars. He wanted to say something. Most of the time these days, words poured out of him. He'd never been a silent boy, but he'd been reserved, quiet. With Neal, however, he'd talked and talked. Being with Neal was like discovering life all over again for the first time. She would talk of something, and somehow it was always a question that they could talk about. They exchanged ideas back and forth. But now, when he felt a need to speak of something more important than any of the many things they shared, he found he was holding his breath. His head was slightly dizzy. He let out his breath with a sigh, knowing that he could not find the words he needed.

Neal turned to look at him. The willow trees hid the sun, and Rick couldn't be sure of the expression in her eyes. The river was darker here. "We'll be there soon," he told her quietly.

"Okay," she said, and smiled. She put the jacket that had lain in the bottom of the boat about her shoulders, and in that gesture Rick saw once more for a moment the separate worlds they lived in. "People are all the same," he had told her, but he wasn't sure that he believed that himself. He wanted to believe that. But the jacket that Neal had left unnoticed in the bottom of the boat was a soft fawn suede. Rick was sure it cost more than any jacket anyone he knew had ever owned. The differences were small, but they were there.

Harley and he had a special place they left the boat. Since they discovered the rowboat abandoned one winter on the bank, washed down from some town far upstream, they had often done just what Rick and Neal had done today. When Rick and Harley floated down the river, you could hear them in the next county, shouting and pushing each other in and just generally kicking back.

The sun was setting far across the fields. A few birds sang in the twilight, and Rick felt a pulling at his heart that he knew was his feelings for Neal, feelings that almost hurt, they ran so deep. He put the oars back in their locks, bent forward and threw his strength into pulling the boat the rest of the way to the small inlet where Harley and he could pick it up later.

Twilight grayed the countryside as Rick

turned into the inlet. He rowed the boat faster toward the beach, feeling it scrape against the river bottom, and let the momentum carry it as far as it would to dry land. He kicked off his sneakers and socks, rolled up his jeans, and leaped out into the icy river water to haul the boat farther in.

Before he knew what she was doing, Neal was in the river up to her bare ankles beside him, hauling on the boat.

"Hey," he said. "You shouldn't do this! This is man's work."

She gave him a good hefty shove at that, and he stumbled backward, almost losing his footing. Regaining his balance, he went back to where she was holding onto the boat by the bow.

"Well," he said, "you think it's not man's work, haul it in, Miss Shaw." He went and walked slowly out of the cold river up the bank, leaving her there, holding onto the boat.

He sat down on the river bank.

"What are you doing?" she asked him, saying each word separately and distinctly.

"Why, I'm waiting here, Miss Shaw, for you to beach the boat," he said innocently.

She took a deep breath. Whatever she was going to reply, she changed her mind. She turned and started pulling on the boat. A worse fear crossed Rick's mind. Suppose she *could* beach the boat by herself? She could control a horse better than any man Rick knew except Kenny.

He got up and went back down to the river, trying not to show his haste. Together, they hauled the boat to safety. Rick reached in and took out both their pairs of shoes and socks. He didn't like the look of triumph on Neal's face as they sat side by side, putting on their sneakers.

But she didn't crow. That was a relief.

"Stubborn little devil, aren't you?" he said as he stood up.

"Determined," she corrected him as he helped her to her feet.

From here they had a short walk over the fields to the road that led into Linden Hill. He led her through the woods that fringed the river. The warm spring day had faded into a cool, quiet night. Rick felt a contentment such as he thought the animals that he knew were nearby must feel. The winter was over, and spring was here. He knew this countryside, every inch of it.

Without knowing quite when he did it, he put his arm about Neal's shoulder. He held her against him in a brotherly way, unselfconsciously, as he helped her up through the woods and out onto the clear, wide fields.

"You love all this, don't you?" Neal asked him.

He nodded. "Yes. I guess a person always loves where they grew up."

He knew he shouldn't have said that. This was Neal's home as much as his, but she didn't know it as he did. She'd been away too long.

"This is going to ruin your shoes," he said ruefully as they walked out onto the field. The heavy mud clung to their sneakers.

"They'll wash," she said, smiling up at him.

Then, as unselfconsciously as they had come together, an awkwardness struck both of them at the same time. Rick's arm felt still around her shoulders, and he knew that she, too, was feeling that she should move away but was afraid to do so for fear of hurting him. They walked a few more yards like that. Rick found that in his mind he was agreeing with Neal; love *was* complicated.

A thin, sickle-shaped moon was rising like a hook against a translucent dark blue sky, and Rick took the opportunity to drop his arm from about Neal's shoulders and point out to her how the moon fit perfectly over the chimneys of Linden Hill, her father's house, scarcely visible in the night. The moon, as it rose into the night looked as if it could lift the house like an ornament and dangle it above the land.

They were both more comfortable than when they were walking by themselves. Some of Rick's good feelings of the day were lost, as always happened when he was about to part with Neal. He put his hands deeper into the pockets of his jeans, leading her out of the rutted field by the shortest route and down onto the highway.

A pickup truck went by loaded with what Rick knew would be the last of the baled hay the farmer would need until next winter. The herd could graze now for the next months. They walked on through the night, the soft silence of the countryside left behind as they came closer to the nearest houses. Cars passed them going in each direction. Rick led Neal across the road so that they were walking facing the traffic and could be seen more clearly.

The gates of Linden Hill were ahead when Rick heard a sound that made his heart turn to ice and his back stiffen. He knew that engine. Brad Rawson's black Charger was coming down the road.

Rick didn't say anything. He kept walking, but he moved so that Neal was well protected, crowding her off the road onto the road's edge so that she looked at him briefly, confused. She, too, saw the black car as it came down the road ahead of them, catching both of them in its beams just before they turned in the driveway of Linden Hill.

Someone shouted something after Rick that was lost in the night.

Neal put her hand on his arm, but it wasn't

the way it had been before when they were walking through the woods; not at all. Before, they had been comfortable together. This was sympathy, and sympathy wasn't what Rick Prescott wanted from Neal Shaw. What Rick Prescott wanted from Neal Shaw was love.

10

He knew what people were thinking. They were thinking that Rick Prescott had caught himself the richest girl in town and was holding on tight. But he didn't care. Neal had said she wanted to feel at home, and he was showing off his home town—their home town.

Linden.

He'd lived here all his life, and he'd never thought much about the place until Kenny and his mom had decided to go south. Then he had been a little sad, but he'd had so much more on his mind, he hadn't thought too much about the town then, either. Now that he was showing Linden to Neal, he saw the little town with new eyes, and he found that he loved the place the way you could only love somewhere that you'd grown up, where every corner, every hill, every house, meant something to you, had a memory of its own, of people who had lived there, things that had happened, summer days spent on river banks and winter mornings pushing through snow to the school bus.

Neal had none of that. Neal had memories. She had memories of Linden, too, but mostly they were memories of where streets led, the memories of a very young child who might someday have to find her way home.

Rick's memories were of things that had happened to him, so they drove everywhere together in the red convertible, Neal behind the wheel and Rick beside her, talking and laughing as he described the time Harley and he spent all day tying a rope to a tree branch over the river, hoping to make a swing, and then when it was done, argued for one more whole day about who was going to swing on it first, and then, when finally they went back the third day, deciding to swing together, found that the farmer who owned the land had come along and sawed the branch off because it was dangerous.

"No," Neal said, laughing.

"Oh, yes," Rick told her. "Right there," and he pointed to the deep pool of water, now swelled with the first runoff of the spring, where they could just see the darker shadowed movement of fish in the depths.

"So what did you do?" Neal asked.

"Took off all our clothes and went swimming, anyway," Rick said.

Neal lay on the grass, looking down at the cool gray water. "You've been so lucky," she murmured.

He had. Rick knew that. These last months had been hard ones for the family, and he saw times ahead for himself when he would have to push for all he was worth to get what he needed, an education. But to hear Neal say that made him feel strange. He thought Neal was the most wonderful girl he had ever met, the most strange and the most mysterious, but he also thought that she was the luckiest, too, not because she was rich but for other reasons. She was bright, and she was beautiful, and the whole world could be hers if she only understood it, but she didn't seem to know that.

People thought she was spoiled. He knew that from the small amount of gossip he heard. He didn't listen to gossip usually because gossip was mostly jealousy, but now they were saying things about him, too.

He didn't care. They didn't know Neal. Sometimes he wondered if Neal knew Neal.

"What are you going to do?" he asked, pulling daisies out of the lush new grass.

"When?" she asked.

Questions like that were exactly what he meant. "Now, tomorrow, next month, in the fall?" he asked.

Her face lost some of its light when he asked those questions. "Toots wants . . ." she began.

But he didn't want to hear what Toots wanted. He had a pretty good idea what Toots wanted. Toots wanted her to hook up with Brad Rawson. "What do *you* want?" he asked.

When he asked direct questions like that, she'd sometimes tried to avoid answering them. She'd drop her head slightly so her long, dark hair fell forward to hide her face, and she'd change the subject. But today she said, "I want to be useful." She almost whispered it, as if it were something she should be ashamed of.

"That's great," he said. "What's wrong with that?"

"Nothing," she said, looking at him defiantly, as though he were the one who was stopping her.

"So?" he said.

"So, daddy's worked so hard for everything," she said, and when she saw that Rick was about to speak, she rushed on. "He really has, and now he thinks he can give me a life like he never had, and he doesn't understand at all that I might not want what he thinks I do."

"It's *your* life," Rick said.

"Not completely," Neal said steadily. "You talk about your mom a lot and how you want her to be proud of you because of all the hard times she's had. It's not so different for Toots. He wants life to be better for me, too."

Rick threw the daisies one by one into the slowly moving pool of the stream and watched them float away in a pattern. Some things, he guessed, you just couldn't explain to people. They either knew them, or they didn't. And the best way to know things was to live them. Maybe the only way.

He showed her his home town, holding back only one place for a reason that wasn't really even clear to him. He showed her where he and Harley used to steal eggs from the chicken coops of local farmers, make little fires in the woods and boil up hard-boiled eggs in the summer. He showed her where he liked to walk alone in the fall so he could watch the quilt of multicolored leaves thrown across the Virginia hills. He showed her his own short cuts through the countryside.

And, of course, he showed her the regular places, like the one movie theater in town and the high school stadium and the municipal swimming pool and the places where kids who had their own cars went to get away from adults; and in all these places he was seen with her.

You couldn't miss that red sports car; everybody saw them and drew their conclusions. Sometimes, driving down a street where people stood watching, Rick would be careful not to catch anyone's look; though he wasn't ashamed to be with Neal, he was somehow embarrassed a little, though he knew he shouldn't be. Let people think what they wanted, he told himself. He and Neal were friends, and he'd never had a friend like Neal. He wanted to spend every moment he could with her, and she seemed to want to do the same with him.

And they talked and talked and talked as Rick had never talked to anyone else. Even when he was alone, he carried on conversations in his mind with Neal, and when he was at school or working, half his attention was somewhere else, with her.

He wanted Neal to know everything that had ever happened in his life, and he wanted to know everything that had ever happened in hers. There didn't seem to be enough time in the day to tell each other everything they had to say. Rick had never been much of a talker, but now he was talking all the time, it seemed. About halfway through something he was saying, he'd see that look he'd come to recognize on Neal's face that she *understood,* understood exactly what he was saying, and that something similar had happened to her, and sure enough, he would barely be stopped before she started talking.

Mind you, what Neal had to tell him happened mostly in London and Paris and New York and boarding school, and almost everything Rick had to tell her happened here in Linden, about two miles from where he was tonight, bent over a carburetor, but that didn't seem to matter much anymore. It was like being one person, having a friendship like this. Getting to know Neal was like discovering that part of him had been missing all his life and finally he had found it.

Ben came out of the office. He looked at Rick's work, nodded appreciatively, and went on to look at the other cars. Ben hadn't said a word about the fact that Neal came around every night on Rick's break and that they sat outside in her car and talked and listened to the radio. Toots had said plenty. Neal told Rick that Toots told her he thought it wasn't ladylike to come down to the garage, but Neal had stood up to him and just kept on coming. She brought him a cold dinner most nights instead of the peanut butter and jelly sandwiches Rick fixed for himself before. Now he sat in the sports car and ate cold chicken and cheese and fruit.

He heard the smooth purr of the sports car drawing up outside and stood up. Ben was watching him through the glass window of his office. Rick went into the locker room, washed up and came out. He signed out for his lunch hour and went out into the car lot.

Neal was waiting far off to one side. He slid in beside her. She had a tape playing in the radio. "Hi," she said.

"What you bring me?" he joked.

"Gee, that's all you want me for, isn't it? Dinner," she said.

He wondered if she knew how he really felt. Sometimes he thought she did. Sometimes he thought that maybe she felt the same way. He would catch her looking at him in a way that wasn't quite how you look at a friend, as though she were assessing him, summing him up or something. But as soon as she caught him looking at her, her expression would change in an instant, and he couldn't really be sure of what he thought he'd seen.

"When I look at you," he said, "I see . . ."

She was wary. Part of their friendship was kidding around.

". . . a chicken sandwich?" he finished hopefully.

"Wrong!" she said. She reached in the back of the seat and brought out a small hamper. From within, she unpacked cold beef, potato salad and a pudding in a white dish. She gave him a linen napkin for his lap and sat there while he ate.

"You don't have to do this, you know," he told her, but he was wolfing down the food, anyway.

"It's no big deal," she said. "I just wait until dinner is over and go in the kitchen and have the cook make up one more plate."

"What did you do all day?" he asked her. They didn't have much time they could spend together, but somehow even the time apart wasn't really apart because they told each other everything they did.

Neal sighed. "Mostly I was . . . a lady," she said.

That was what Toots wanted for her, Neal told Rick. He wanted her to be "a lady."

"Sounds good to me," Rick said, thinking about his own mom. His own mom was a lady—no doubt about it—but that wasn't what Toots meant. Toots meant that he didn't want his daughter to work.

Neal said, "Sometimes I just wish . . ." She didn't finish.

"What?" Rick prompted.

"Well, I just wish I was sort of like you," she said, looking directly at him.

If she'd said she wanted to grow blue hair, Rick couldn't have been more surprised. "Me?" he asked.

"You know how to *do* things," Neal said. "You can fix cars, you can look after yourself, you're allowed . . . you're allowed to grow up."

Growing up, Rick thought, hadn't been any

trouble at all. He hadn't had any choice. When
he thought about that and all the problems his
mom and Kenny had in the last year and how
bad they had felt that Rick had to stay behind
and work to finish school, he got a little angry at
Neal.

He sighed and looked out the side window of
the car. Way across the parking lot, he saw a
small figure come out of the main building and
stand, hand on hips, staring at the red car.
"Toots," he said.

Neal followed the direction of his look. She
didn't say anything.

The small flash of anger died down. In its
place came a type of sadness. He always hated
to part with Neal. There was always so much
more to say. He had so much to tell her and so
much he wanted to know. "I've got to go," he
said.

Neal packed away the remains of the dinner
she had brought him. Rick got out of the car.
He went around to her window.

"Tomorrow?" she asked.

Rick stood looking at her in her beautiful car.
"There's a place I want to show you," he said.
They were so different, Neal and he, and suddenly he knew he had to show her the one place
in Linden he'd held back, kept for himself, as
though when he gave her that, she would have
all he had to give except the one thing she didn't

want, his love. Once she had been there, she would know everything there was to know about him.

"Where?" she asked.

"I'll show you tomorrow," he said.

It was raining when she picked him up, the heavy earth-quenching rain of late spring. She didn't ask him where they were going, but followed his directions off the main roads and down the back lanes.

They rode in comfortable warmth together, wrapped in the sounds of the music and the insistent background drumming of the rain. Rick felt a twinge of something like pain as he recognized the old landmarks, the narrow bridge over the creek, now swelled with the spring runoff, the field where his mom had run the horse she loved so much before she'd had to sell it, the stand of birch trees waving in the wind and rain where he'd built his first tree house.

"This is where you used to live, isn't it?" Neal said.

"Yes," he admitted. It was somehow important now that she understood how he'd grown up. He saw the house up ahead through the trees and felt a quick regret, but it was too late to change directions.

Neal was looking out her side window at the old shed to the side of the house where Kenny had kept his work tools, and Rick saw it as it must look through her eyes. Kenny had taken everything that he needed and left the rest behind where he'd dropped it; untidy, empty nail cans, the wood bench he couldn't fit on the trailer left to the weather, an old tire.

Confused feelings went through Rick, shame at the condition of the area and then anger that he didn't understand. He wouldn't apologize for this place. His mom had loved this house. But to Neal, he was sure, this must look like a slum.

The house was directly ahead; gray, plain, nothing special unless you had lived there. He turned off the ignition. The radio died with it. The rain sounded louder, and as the windshield wipers stopped, the image of the house and the surroundings was slowly hidden by a film of rain.

"Do you have a key?" Neal asked.

"No," he said. "But I know how to get in."

"Will you show it to me?"

"It's nothing special," he said. "I don't know why I brought you here."

She looked at him. "I'd like to see it," she said.

He'd brought her out here, but now he wished he hadn't. She'd say polite things about the house, but he knew that living as she did, this must look like a dump.

Before he could think of a way to say no, Neal opened the car door and got out. She ran to the front steps and stood in the shelter of the porch roof. Rick got out and followed her up to the door. He'd come home through this door from school most of his life. In the winter, there'd be a light behind the glass, and in the summer the screen door would be up and the inside door open, the radio playing and his mom cooking dinner. Even empty, the old place looked inviting, the way an old sweater you'd half forgotten you owned, turning up in the bottom of a drawer at just the right moment when you needed it, made you feel good. He reached up and slammed the door with the flat of his hand right at the top, and as it always had, it popped open.

"Magic," he said to Neal.

He put his arm around her as he led her inside. He did it without thought, and she didn't move away. The old kitchen looked pretty sad, he had to admit, with the yellow walls needing a new coat of paint and the green linoleum, which had been his mom's big purchase four years before, coming up in the corner. Rick could remember the day he and Kenny had worked to put it down.

He sighed. Neal's arm came about his waist, and she hugged him gently. He was grateful for the gesture, friendly and reassuring at the exact moment he needed it. He looked down at her. She looked so young, so beautiful. He tried to remember the girl he'd seen a few weeks before driving furiously along the back roads, but she seemed to be fading. Here beside him was a young girl who was . . . nice.

"What are you smiling at?" she asked suspiciously.

"I was just thinking," he said.

"About what?"

He didn't know how she'd take it. He said, "You are a nice person, Neal Shaw. You know that?"

The light in her eyes changed, dulled, and for a second he thought she was annoyed, but then he saw a film on her eyes that he knew couldn't be tears but was mighty close. "I'm sorry if I've upset you," he said.

"You haven't upset me, Rick," she said softly. "That's maybe the"—she searched for the words—"*nicest* thing anyone's ever said to me." She squeezed him again about the waist, but it was the hug of a friend or a sister and a brother, reassuring, comfortable. Rick, who wanted more than anything to take her in both his arms and hold her tight to him, had to drop his arm from about her shoulder, because if they stood like that much longer, he was going to make a move he'd regret.

He led Neal through the house. He tried the switch in the hall, but the electricity was off. So she moved closer to him as he walked confidently through the rooms. He showed her the bedrooms—the bigger bedroom where his mom and Kenny had slept, the room for the twins, and then his own room, right at the end of the hall. You could still see the faded places of the wallpaper where his school pennants had hung.

They walked back to the living room. The rain was really coming down hard now, hammering on the roof like an artillery battalion. Speech was impossible. The living room was so small in the dark, the big oil stove Kenny had put in when the heating bills got too high two winters ago, awkward and out of proportion, but Rick could remember how much they had enjoyed that stove when it arrived. They would heat that up in the evening, and as they watched television, the room would get so hot you had to take off your sweaters, even though it was two feet deep with snow outside. Kenny would sit in his undershirt and watch television. Some nights it got so hot in there it drove them out of the room, and they'd have to open a door to let in some winter air. But that stove kept the whole house warm through the night. No more waking up to freezing rooms and floors like an ice rink, no more cold bathrooms.

Rick and Neal stood side by side in the living room, looking out the big front window at the trees and the soggy grass. Rick could smell her perfume in the room, and as she turned, he felt her hair brush against his cheek; without thinking, he very gently pulled her closer until he could almost feel her heart beat against his. She looked up at him, her eyes wide, her lips parted as though she were about to say something, but the drumming of the rain filled the house with a roar. Rick knew that he was going to lean down and kiss her, because no matter what their deal had been, he loved her, but as he knew that, a light swept across the front of the house, revealing them in the window, and another car swung around the drive onto the high ground, out of the way of the mud and rain. Neal moved away.

Rick saw the real estate agent who had sold the house get out of his car and run for the back door that Rick had left open.

"Anybody here?" he called, though he knew there was because the red sports car was sitting right out there.

Rick shouted back, "Here, Mr. Brown." The real estate agent appeared in the door to the small living room.

"Rick?" the agent said uncertainly.

"Yeah, Mr. Brown," Rick said. "It's me."

The agent looked at Neal and then back at Rick. "You forget something?" the agent asked.

"No, no," Rick said, looking about the

room. "I remembered everything. Just wanted to show the old place to a friend."

Nobody said anything for a second. Then Neal said, "We have to get back." She nodded politely to the real estate man and went out.

The real estate man said, "I just came out to see that everything was all right. You know how that creek can rise."

"Seems okay today," Rick said.

"Right," the man agreed. "But the spring runoff—you never know."

Rick admitted you didn't and said good-bye. When he got out to the car, Neal was sitting in the passenger seat. She didn't look at him, but the car keys were in the ignition. Rick got in and sat behind the steering wheel without speaking. He put both hands on the wheel. He knew something had changed, something important, but he wasn't sure what it was. He was afraid to ask Neal, afraid that his words would sound clumsy. She was facing away from him, looking out her side window.

The real estate man had come out on the porch. He was staring reflectively toward the red car. Rick had a pretty good idea what he was thinking. He was thinking what everyone else was thinking: that Rick Prescott had lucked out, that he'd found the richest girl in town. For the first time in his life, Rick understood how it was different for the rich; nobody let you just be.

Well, he couldn't help what people thought. He sighed, turned the key in the ignition and carefully backed the car out of the driveway. Neal still hadn't said a word. He headed for the main highway. The creek was rising, as the real estate man had said. A sheen of water polished the road. Rick drove carefully, feeling the car under his hands. He took them through the outskirts of town and up into the suburbs, heading for Linden Hill. The rain was coming down more heavily now. The windshield wiper swept back and forth, leaving a thick layer of moisture in its path.

Rick peered forward. Neal reached out and turned on the radio. He looked at her hand on the knob as country music filled the car, then back at the road, and in that second he knew that he had misjudged. The car started to skid with its rear wheels, slowing at first, then more rapidly as the mud took a grip, spinning the car around once, then again. The first blow hit the car at the rear left fender, jolting both of the riders in the car, and Rick reached out with his right arm to hold Neal, but the car spun in the opposite direction, and he needed both hands. He let go of Neal as the car hit the second, large object, a tree hidden in the torrential rain, on the right. They were sliding downhill now; then the car took one last wrenching blow and came to a stop. In the awful moment after the accident, when the only sound was the thrashing of the rain on the roof and the whine of the dying engine, Neal whispered with dread the very words that were in Rick's mind. "What will Toots say?"

11

Toots said, "How are you going to pay for it?"

The red sports car, twisted beyond recognition, sat outside the showroom window, a mute monument to the accident.

"The car wasn't insured?" Rick asked. He felt a great hopelessness, as though nothing that could happen now could really touch him. He hadn't seen Neal since the accident two days ago.

"Not for you to drive," Toots said.

After the accident, Rick had walked four miles in the rain to find a telephone booth. Neal had stayed crouched under a hedge out of the rain. The car lay on its side, both fenders, front and back, crumpled; part of the transmission had been torn away, leaving a smear of oil on the sodden grass. The tow truck from Uncle Toots' Carnival of Cars picked Rick up as he was walking back, and by the time he got to the accident, Toots was there, too.

Neal had been sitting inside the white Lincoln town car, wet and unhappy. Toots, wrapped in a brown raincoat that looked as though it belonged to someone else, hadn't said a word when the tow truck came upon the ruined sports car. He merely looked at Rick in contempt, turned and got in his car, and drove Neal off.

Rick waited for the tow-truck driver to hook chains under the wreck, helping as best he could, then went back to the garage with the car. It seemed everybody in the garage and at the dealership already knew what had happened. They stood about in little groups to watch as the evidence pulled in.

Ben was the only one who showed any sympathy. He came over to Rick as he got out of the tow truck and said, "Come on, I'll drive you home."

Rick followed Ben to his own camper. On the way to Adele's, the only thing Ben said was "Don't be too hard on yourself, kid."

Rick couldn't answer. A whole dream had slid into the ditch with the car. He didn't know what he felt. He felt cold and lonely, sad and unhappy, angry all at once. He wanted to say,

"It isn't fair," but that was what kids said, and he wasn't a kid anymore.

He got out without a word, went inside, took a shower and went to bed. He didn't sleep. He tried to calm himself, but the anger grew and grew. He wanted to get up and call Neal to see if she was all right, but he knew that if he did that, he wouldn't be allowed to speak to her, and he also knew that Toots would do everything in his power never to let Rick see Neal again.

Rick felt helpless. Neal lived in one world, and he lived in another, and she had wanted to be his friend, and he . . . he loved her. He knew that. But maybe people were right when they had said that the two worlds couldn't mix.

At that thought, the anger flowed through him again. He tried calming himself by doing what he did when he was a kid, by thinking about good things in the past, summers he loved at the lake, his grandmother, the fences he built around the old property with Kenny. Outside his bedroom, the house was quiet. Adele and Harley knew what had happened and were leaving Rick to work out his own troubles.

He didn't go to school the next day, or to work. Ben understood when Rick phoned in. "Take your time, Rick," he said. "The job will be here when you come back." Rick knew that was Ben's own judgment. Ben didn't say a lot, but Toots respected Ben, and Rick was sure that while Toots would have fired him, Ben was insisting that Rick be kept on. Toots needed Ben. Ben ran the machine shop smoothly, and the shop was important to the whole operation.

While Adele and Harley were away during the day, Rick sat around the house, thinking. You could kid yourself as much as you like, he told himself, but a girl like Neal is not for you. Ever since he was a kid, he had made a practice of trying to tell the truth to himself. He knew he wasn't as smart as many guys, he knew he wasn't the best jock around, or the best-looking, and he knew that Kenny and his mom lived like regular middle-class working people, and he had never been ashamed of any of it or felt that he was any the less for all of that until Neal came along. That was what made it all so hard. He had been proud of himself and his family. They didn't have all the things that Toots did or Rawson did, but they were good, decent people, and his mom had always said that was the best you could be. But now he found that there was something else, too. Money—not just money to pay bills and have big houses, but money that put people into different worlds, and much as they liked each other, it was as though they were on either sides of a creek, with the spring runoff raging down between them, and though they could shout across that creek, they couldn't reach each other.

"Well, now you know it, Prescott," he told himself finally. The pain of losing Neal, as he knew now he would, when he had felt that he was just on the verge of becoming more than friends, stabbed at him, but he told himself to get real, grow up and go on.

He had things to do in his life—like pay for the sports car, which was a mass of twisted metal prominently displayed in front of the showroom. "I'll work for you," Rick said, facing Toots across his desk the next day.

Toots let out a sound that might have been a laugh or a sigh gone wrong. "Son," he told him, "if I told you what that car cost, you'd know how crazy that offer is. That car cost more than you'll make in a year for a long time to come."

There had to be something more coming, and Rick knew what it was. He didn't want to hear it, and though he had already made up his mind not to see Neal anymore because it would hurt too much and be hopeless, anyway, he wasn't going to allow Toots to make him say it. He wasn't going to sell out what he had left of his friendship with Neal for a debt repayment on a car.

He said, "I'll be gone soon," and let Toots sit there behind his desk, letting the words and what they really meant sink in. A gleam of what might have been anger flashed across Toots' eyes.

Toots let Rick stand there in front of his desk

for a while while he first looked at him, then out the window at the wreck. Finally, all he did was nod and turn to the papers on his desk. Rick thought that Toots had a lot to say, too, and that Toots was afraid to say some of it. Probably for the first time in his life, too, Toots was shutting up.

Rick left the office and walked out through the showroom. Silence fell on the little groups of salesmen as he passed. The girl at the reception desk looked at him, then down at her typewriter. In the garage, Ben told him that he was back on the night shift, showed him his work and went back to his office. The other mechanics left him alone.

That suited Rick fine. He did his work at the garage mechanically, his hands, as they often did, taking on a life of their own so that his thoughts could float away among old memories of his childhood, the house in the country, Kenny, his own father. He tried hard not to think at all, just to work, but these memories seemed to need thinking about because they pushed forward into his mind. Then, suddenly, without warning, Neal's image would be with them. When that happened, when Neal's face appeared in his memory, his breath would literally stop for a second, and he could feel a real pain. He had to stop the work he was doing on a fan belt because he had a lump in his throat. That time, he put down the tools he was working with and walked out into the night, warmer now that spring was edging toward summer, and stood alone in the dark, looking at the place where he and Neal had dinner in the car every night.

Then Rick went back into the shop, took up his tools again and finished the job he was working on. That was what his life was really about, he reminded himself; fan belts and school, not daydreams and beautiful girls who lived in places that might have been other countries, their lives so different from his.

His shift ended, and he changed his clothes and washed up.

The night was warm. Rick walked along the road on the way home, listening to cars in the distance. The kids at school were getting ready for graduation. There were still two weeks to go, but they acted as though high school was over, which it was, except for a few classes and the dance.

Most of the kids already knew what they were going to do. Some were going to work, and some were going to college. The college scores had been in for a long time, and every day someone got accepted somewhere else.

Rick still hadn't sent in his application to the junior college down in Florida. His scores were good enough, as were his marks, and he was sure that he would get a good personal reference from his teachers, but the thought of leaving, of next year, of all that, dragged him down. He put it off.

He was boring to be around, he knew. He could tell from the way the kids looked at him in school, sort of half sorry for him, half impatient. He was a ghost at the feast.

And the truth was he thought they were right. They'd worked for twelve years to get to this moment. They were going to graduate and go on with their lives, their adult lives. He didn't have any right to drag them down with his own troubles.

So he stayed off by himself, going to school, going to work, going home along the lanes that he loved at night, listening in the summer silence to the sound of small animals and the flight of birds.

One day, people wrote, you got over your first love. The pain stopped, and you looked back and wondered why you had made such a fuss of it. But he couldn't believe it.

He saw that Adele's bedroom light was on as he came up the lane. He thought maybe Adele understood. She hadn't said anything, but from the way she looked at him, he knew that she understood that he was hurt, and worse, angry because he never really had a chance to love Neal.

Harley had left a cheese sandwich and a glass of milk out for Rick. He ate them standing up in the kitchen. The phone on the wall looked larger than usual. Nowadays, when he saw a phone, all he wanted to do was reach out and dial Neal, but that would only make everything worse.

As he went down the hall, Adele called from her room. "Rick?"

"Yeah." He stopped in her door.

Adele was sitting up in bed reading. She read one book on love after another. She always looked now as though she wanted to talk to him, to tell him something, but the last thing Rick wanted was to talk about what he was feeling. If he started to talk about it, he didn't know what might happen. He was bursting with feelings that he didn't understand. He felt pressured inside like gas in a piston chamber. He dreaded the spark that might ignite them, bursting forth in meaningless ends and maybe even tears. He was unraveling inside. How could he explain it was more than a wrecked car and a lost friend. He had lost someone who seemed like the other half of himself.

"Everything okay?" Adele asked hesitantly.

"Everything's fine," Rick said.

"Harley says you're not going to the graduation dance."

"No," Rick said, letting out with a sigh the breath that he had been holding in. "No, I thought I'd sit that one out."

"You should go, Rick," Adele said. "Harley's going." What she meant was *"Even* Harley's going." Harley's going to a dance was as rare as a green cat.

"Yeah, well, I still think I'll sit it out," Rick said, trying to throw in a smile because it wasn't Adele's fault he felt so bad. "Harley can dance for both of us. I've got to save money for the bus ride."

Adele looked at him sympathetically, but she didn't offer any more advice. He went on down to his room. The conversation with Adele had helped in some small way. He had to save money for the bus trip, he said, and in saying it, somehow that trip south to join Kenny and his mom and the family had become real. He'd been putting off thinking about that until now, and he realized that he had been putting it off because buying that ticket would be admitting his friendship with Neal was really over. Neal and he had been friends; then he had broken up the friendship with the car, not because she didn't want to see him but because that twisted pile of metal showed that her world and his world were just too far apart.

Now he opened the bottom drawer of his desk and took out the brochures that his mom had sent up about the community college. The college didn't look so bad, he had to admit as he examined them; maybe the buildings were pink and the kids looked as if they had majored in surfing at two, but the academic credits were good. He began to fill out the application, and he kept on until it was finished. Then he sealed the envelope and propped it up against his books. He changed quickly, climbed into bed and switched off the bedside lamp. The open shade let in the ghostly light of the early-summer moon. He looked at the faintly luminous envelope across the room.

Florida wouldn't be so bad, he thought. He'd have a part-time job and go to school and get an education and . . . he left it there. Before, he used to think he'd go to school and get an education and meet someone and have a family, and he'd think about the type of person he'd meet and where they'd live and what the children might be like, but he'd already met the type of person he wanted, the person *he* loved, and he couldn't imagine that he could ever love anyone else.

After a while, he fell asleep.

He saw her once, unexpectedly, when he had gone to the shopping center with Adele to choose a small birthday present for his young stepsister. They were in the children's department, and Adele was helping him pick out a blouse for Helen when, looking up, he saw Neal in the distance through the crowd of shoppers. His heart stopped, literally, his knees went weak, and he felt a mild nausea overcome him. In his mind, she had stayed as beautiful as he had always thought her, but the sight of her there, real, across the store, shook him. She was everything he remembered and more, for just then, as he stared, she turned, and across that great distance their eyes seemed to fix upon each other as though there were not another person in the whole shopping center. He saw her eyes widen with surprise and what might have been accusation, but he couldn't be sure right then. People moved across their line of vision, and the noise of the store that had seemed to die away for that one moment of shock flooded back, and when the people moved on, Neal was gone.

"You like this one or this one?" Adele was saying, holding up two blouses, one green, one pink.

But Rick shook his head. "Doesn't matter," he said.

"You all right?" Adele said. "You look like you've seen a ghost."

"I don't like so many people around," Rick lied. "Let's get out of here. You choose for me."

Adele chose the green, and they had it wrapped to be mailed and left as fast as they could.

"You look pale," Adele said when they were driving home in her car. "That Florida sun will do you good. You've been working too hard."

"Virginia has sun," Rick murmured.

"Not like Florida," Adele said. "You wait

and see; you'll love Florida. You'll forget all about us up here in Virginia."

"No, I won't," Rick said, and the edge in his voice made Adele turn to look at him once, quickly, before they drove on home in silence.

"You're accepted!" Rick's mom's voice was filled with pride. No one in his family had ever gone to college.

"You got it already?" he asked. He had sent in his application with his transcripts and school references three weeks before, giving the Florida address of his mom and Kenny.

"I called up!" she said.

"Oh, mom," Rick groaned.

"Don't oh, mom me," she told him. "I called up and checked. Oh, Rick, I'm so proud of you. I'm so happy. You'll be here soon and going to college."

The sun shone through the kitchen window, throwing a square of yellow light on the pale-gray linoleum of Adele's kitchen. He was proud of himself, too, he had to admit. He was going to college, and it was true he missed his mom and the long talks with Kenny, and even his little stepbrother and stepsister, who drove him crazy most of the time when they were around.

But he would miss Virginia, too. He'd stopped thinking about Neal so much. He had heard through the school grapevine that she had gone to a movie with Brad Rawson and that he had been over to the house on Linden Hill again for dinner, but people had stopped looking so strangely at Rick, and nobody talked to him about Neal. The silences that happened when he walked up to groups had stopped. People thought he'd gotten over Neal, he guessed, and even Brad Rawson had stopped the strutting around that he had done in the days after the accident. Brad Rawson had other things on his mind these days. His marks weren't so great, and he had been told he had to make up one course in the summer semester to get into the agricultural college.

And, of course, he was seeing Neal, Rick knew, so he didn't have to make any big point of things anymore.

"I guess you're having a beautiful Virginia spring, now, huh?" his mom asked wistfully. She missed her old home, too, he knew, but you had to go on, as she reminded him sometimes in her letters, and Florida was lovely too, though different.

"Almost gone," Rick told her. "The apple blossoms are great, but the rains have stopped."

"You know how we tell the seasons down here?" his mom asked.

"No." He heard that "we." She was settling in.

"The snowbirds go north. A snowbird is

someone who comes down for the winter and goes home when the weather gets better up north."

"This snowbird will be down soon," he told her.

"People say it's nicer with the tourists gone. We'll have the beaches to ourselves. Think of that, Rick."

"I do," he told her. "You hug the kids for me, huh? And what the heck; hug Kenny for me."

"I'll do that," his mom said before she rang off. And then she added, "Rick I'm so proud of you."

"Not all my doing," he told her. "I was just raised right, I guess."

"That's true," she told him, and then rang off.

After he hung up, he went out into the garden. The cat from next door was crouched in the shade of a chinaberry bush just breaking into bud, watching a nest of baby birds up in the boughs of the flowering maple.

The cat reminded him of Brad Rawson. He threw a stone in its direction, scaring it off, as the mother robin returned with a long, juicy worm hanging out of both sides of its mouth and the tiny robin heads stuck up, beaks wide, crying tiny little cries of joy.

He was proud of himself, too, he admitted.

He had gotten into college. He had set goals and achieved them. But still he felt a great emptiness when he thought of that ruined car that Toots had left sitting out on the lot as a reminder to Rick that he had a long way to go before he could deserve someone like Neal Shaw.

Neal Shaw. The pain was dimming as time passed. He still loved her; he knew that, but it was easier when he didn't see her. He woke up every morning thinking about her, and his last thought every night was of her. He thought maybe she would call him, and for the first weeks, each time the telephone rang, his heart would miss a beat, and he would try not to listen, not to hope, but it never was Neal, except maybe once—when walking through the kitchen at Adele's, the phone rang just as he came abreast of it, as though it personally wanted him to pick it up.

He did. "Hello," he said, and there was a long silence on the other end of the line. He was afraid to speak into the silence, afraid that if it was Neal, he would frighten her away. The silence stretched on for nearly a minute. Then he said, "Hello, hello?" but still there was no answer, just the soft singing of the empty wire stretching away into the countryside and then, softly, the sound of the phone at the other end being hung up.

He stood by the phone at Adele's for a few more minutes, hoping that it might ring again.

When it didn't, he walked away toward his room, all his old feelings flooding back, the longing for Neal, the emptiness, the loss that he had felt when they were first apart. He tried studying, but he couldn't concentrate.

He went back to the kitchen at a run, picked up the phone and dialed the house on Linden Hill before he could let his mind think. He heard the rings, deliberately blanking out his reason, and then the maid's voice said, "Shaw residence," and all the common sense that had kept him silent and away from Linden Hill came back in one moment, and he muttered, "Wrong number," and hung up.

In his room, he lay down on his bed with his arms behind his head, staring at the ceiling, waiting for the pain to go away again, and for the first time he was reconciled to going to Florida. He couldn't stay here in Linden where he might at any time see Neal, might hear her voice, might see her. He had to go away. And he would; as soon as he had graduated, he would go, as had been his original plan.

So when Harley finally said, "What about the prom?" which was Harley's way of cajoling Rick into going, even going stag, since this was the end of their high school years together, Rick said, "Sorry, buddy. I'm going to sit this one out," in such a way that Harley, a good friend, left him alone and didn't bring it up again.

And on the night of the prom, Rick left school when the other kids did, but while they rushed off to get ready for the dance, Rick went to work as usual.

12

Ben watched as Rick carefully wiped clean each of the tools he had used that night. Ben had to know the prom was on at the school; in a town as small as Linden, a cat stopping to scratch itself as it crossed the road was news. But Ben hadn't said anything when Rick had said he'd work his regular night shift.

Now everyone was gone except Ben and Rick. Uncle Toots' Carnival of Cars was still, in principle, open, but almost nobody ever came in after midnight to buy a car unless they were drunk or desperate because they'd held up a bank. After midnight, two lot boys kept the place open just so the slogan could be kept true.

"You want a ride?" Ben asked.

"I think I'll walk," Rick said. The night

outside was warm. Even Harley was at the dance. Rick didn't feel like getting back to the house to talk to Adele.

"Just pull the last door," Ben said, and went out.

Rick took his time arranging his tools on the bench. He liked things neat. Kenny, as a carpenter, had taught him that. "If you leave things neat," he could hear Kenny's voice saying in his mind, "then they're there when you need them." Kenny was a good man. He was glad his mom had found Kenny. He tried to think what it would be like to be down in Florida with them, but he couldn't get excited about the thought. "If you take care of business," Toots' voice said in his mind in a grating echo of Kenny's, "the rest takes care of itself." There, at least, Toots was right for once.

Rick went into the locker room and stripped off his grease-stained overalls. He tried to figure in the mirror if all this had taught him anything. He looked pretty much the same—blond hair, streaked with a bit more oil tonight, maybe, but other than that, the same old Rick Prescott. He felt real different inside, not bad exactly but changed, as though nothing would ever be the same again. Adele had said, "You'll get over it. You're young." He couldn't believe her. He didn't want to believe her. He didn't think he'd ever feel about anyone else the way he had felt about Neal—the way he still felt about Neal, his heart reminded him with a tug—and he didn't think he wanted to. "Work" is the answer, Toots had said about something weeks before when he was strutting around Linden Hill giving another of his lectures on life to whoever was present, and again, much as Rick hated to admit it, there was some truth in what he said. When Rick was working hard, he could lose himself in what he was doing, in the pleasure of doing something well—fixing an engine, working with Kenny on the split-rail fences around the property before it was sold, putting together a toy for his younger stepbrother and stepsister.

But that only lasted a short time; then all his feelings for Neal would come rushing back— how she had looked when they were talking, the way her hair fell across her face as she leaned forward when she was trying to buy time to think before she answered some question, her perfume—and that was like being hit deep down in the stomach with a fist.

He took a deep breath, turned off the light and went out into the garage.

He liked the silence; he liked the way the bays were neatly lined up, the cars lowered for safety. He went around switching off the power, and then, when he was sure that everything was shut for the night, he went to the last door, pressed the button and stepped out into the warm Virginia night before the door lowered itself on its engine.

"I used to do that," a familiar voice said nearby, startling Rick.

Toots stood in the shadow near his big white Lincoln town car.

"I used to like to make sure everything was shut down for the night. Wouldn't believe anyone else. Used to wake up some nights sure that something was wrong and drive on down to the lot to see if everything was the way it was meant to be. Not this lot, of course," he said, looking out at the acres of brightly lit cars. "Other lot, small one at first, later bigger, then one day . . ." His gesture took in his kingdom of cars, the Carnival of Cars. "Yeah," he said, looking at Rick, "you remind me of myself."

Rick thought that might be the single most insulting thing anyone had ever said to him, but he was too tired to think of an answer, either rude or polite. And he needed the job, he had to remind himself again. He needed the job for a little while longer.

"Had to do everything myself," Toots said.

Rick put his hands in his pockets, facing Toots. Toots hadn't come out here to tell Rick he reminded him of himself.

For a while, neither of them said anything. Rick looked at Toots, and he seemed to be seeing him for the first time. In Rick's mind, Toots was a joke, a bad joke, but what he saw in front of him was a very, very little man and not a very happy one.

"You're a jerk, you know," Toots said.

At first, Rick wasn't sure that he had heard right. Then he thought maybe he had said that himself instead of Toots, since that was what he was thinking.

"I don't get paid to listen to this," Rick heard himself say. No job was worth it. He could get by somehow. He didn't have to listen to this.

"I'm not talking as your boss," Toots said, crossing his arms and his ankles as he leaned against the car. He looked like some small leprechaun who had stolen a car. "As a boss, I'm lucky to have you. Maybe I don't say that, but I know it. You're good, Rick Prescott. You're damn good. But you're dumb."

Rick took a step toward Toots.

Toots didn't move a muscle. Whatever Rick might think of Toots, he was no coward.

"You're gonna lose the girl you want because you're too proud," Toots said.

Rick listened to the sounds of the night. He heard a car far off in the distance screeching on tires, coming from the dance probably, and he had one quick image of Brad Rawson's reckless driving, and then, in the silence, the call of one of the lot boys to the other. "You're something; you really are," he said to Toots.

"You think I'm sort of a fool, don't you?" Toots said. He still hadn't moved.

"No," Rick said. "No, not a fool, Toots." That was the first time he'd ever called Toots by his nickname. Until this moment, he'd called him "Mr. Shaw."

"I started with nothing . . ." Toots began, but Rick turned away before he got any further.

"I've got to go," Rick said.

"No, you listen," Toots ordered, and Rick stood with his back to Toots, but he didn't go anywhere. "I want my girl safe," Toots said.

Rick turned. "You think she's safe with that maniac?" he asked curiously.

Toots had undone his arms. He still leaned against the car, but he stared at the ground. "She's not with him," he said.

Rick's heart seemed to stop. He couldn't speak.

Toots looked up. "All I wanted was for her to be safe. You understand? I started from nothing . . . No, no, you listen . . ." he said, as though he could read the change of expression on Rick's face at the old song coming out again. "And I won't be around to look after her forever, and I want her safe. So . . ."

The sigh that escaped Rick was more sadness than relief. "Did it ever occur to you," he asked, "that maybe she could make her own decisions? Did it ever occur to you, Toots, that she could take care of herself?"

"She has," Toots told him.

Rick waited.

Toots was struggling with a decision. "She's at home," he said finally. "I think maybe she would like to see you." Something close to a smile crossed his face in the warm night. "She sure doesn't want to see anyone else. She won't even talk to me."

Rick had to smile. "Good sense, that girl," he said.

"Must be from her mother," Toots admitted ruefully. "Her father's as dumb as a mule."

Suddenly, the night seemed to be filled with possibilities. Rick could almost like this foolish little man in front of him. Heck, he admitted, he *did* like Toots. But still he had to protest. "I am not like you," he said.

"Not if you're smart enough to go up there and admit maybe you were wrong," Toots said. "I never could apologize. Lonely being right all the time."

Rick looked in the direction of Linden Hill. The time was way after midnight. "Here," Toots said, "take my car." He threw the keys to the Lincoln at Rick, who, out of sheer mule-headed stubbornness of his own, wanted to protest, but he reached out and snatched them from the air.

"You sure?" Rick asked.

"I got lots of cars," Toots pointed out. "If I'm not careful, that's all I'm going to have."

Toots stood away from the car. Rick made his decision and walked slowly toward the car. His heart was racing as though he had run a hundred yards at top speed. "Toots . . ." he said, starting to thank Toots.

But Toots was walking away toward the front of the lot, and Rick had some idea of all the feelings that must be churning through the little man who loved his daughter so much but didn't know how to show that love any other way except to throw money at her.

Rick got in the car, turned on the ignition and sat still. For once, though he was again in one of the Shaw cars, an expensive machine, he didn't feel poor or inferior or any of the feelings that had made him think he was wrong for Neal, that his life was so different, the paths he had to follow leading in such a different direction from hers. This was a car like any other, no different really from Harley's old heap. A machine to take you from one place to the next.

And the next place he wanted to be was Linden Hill, and right away. He backed out of the lot, turned the big car in a neat three-point turn and headed out of town. The dance was breaking up. He passed kids from school hot rodding down the highway, high on good times and the knowledge that school was almost over for them, but they couldn't have felt any better than he did. He lowered the window to let in the warm early-summer air, bringing with it the last of the apple blossoms' perfume and the dark, loamed air of the fields, ready tilled to be sown.

The gates to Linden Hill were open. He remembered his feelings the day he had run away from dinner. Some of those same feelings were coming back now. His courage was waning as he saw the big house through the trees. The lights in most of the lower rooms were out, and all the second floor except for one window was dark.

Suppose this was all another of Toots' crazy ideas, Rick thought. Maybe Toots was wrong. Maybe it wasn't because of Rick at all that Neal was home. He drew up in front of the house and killed the engine. He found his hands were damp. He wiped them on his jeans, then all of a sudden realized that he'd just worked a four-hour shift in a grease pit. He looked again at his face in the rear-view mirror and saw that it hadn't changed any since he checked it in the locker room at the garage. An oil streak in his hair, a smudge on his face. He looked at his hands, clean but rough.

He swallowed hard. The walk to the door of the house seemed the longest he'd ever taken. He pressed the bell and heard the chimes ring inside.

For some minutes, no one answered the door. A wind blew in off the fields. Down at the stables, a colt neighed. Rick was about to turn away, his excitement and nervousness turning to anger, when abruptly Neal stood there before him.

"Did you forget . . ." She had come down to open the door herself, thinking that Toots had come home late without his key. At the sight of Rick, she fell silent.

Rick's mouth was dry. "Uuhh . . ." he said. He felt awkward, huge, dirty, ugly. Neal looked fragile and beautiful. She wore no makeup and was dressed in a gray cotton sweatsuit, her hair held back from her face with a tortoise-shell band. She was barefoot.

Blank-faced, she stared at him as though he were an enemy. "I was just getting ready for bed," she said finally, and then taking hold of a piece of the gray cloth, she shook her head as though she had to explain the sweatsuit. "I've always slept in sweatsuits, since I was . . ." She stopped.

Rick started to step back. "I shouldn't have come," he said. But then he knew, knew more than he had ever known anything, that this was his last chance, that he had to speak now or they would be . . . They might be friends again someday, but they'd never be anything more. He knew what he was going to say even before he said it, heard the words floating in his mind as they rose up in his throat, and then, worse, he felt his eyes film over. "I miss you," he said.

The breath seemed to go out of Neal Shaw. She used her old familiar trick of looking down so that her hair covered her face, and Rick thought that he had lost her, anyway; he'd come here and made his pitch, but it made no difference. But she looked up, and when she spoke, she closed her eyes part way, as though blinking away troubles. Her words were ordinary, but to Rick they brought hope. He wouldn't allow his mind to go any further than that. "Let me get some shoes," she said.

While she was upstairs, he stood in the huge, brightly lit hall trying to keep his mind blank, his feelings calm. The house was as beautiful as always—fresh flowers in large vases, everything spotlessly clean, everything . . . everything rich. But it was just a house tonight, a big house but just a house. His own smudged face, reflected at him from the gilt mirror, looked tense. Neal was back in moments, still wearing the sweatsuit but with a scarf around her neck and white tennis shoes on her feet.

Outside, the stars domed the night. Rick and Neal walked side by side into the garden, both thinking their own thoughts. She led him through the symmetrical flower beds where they had first walked and up the rise where they had stood that night months ago looking down across the countryside coming back to life.

Tonight the moon hung over a velvet landscape of white fences and blooming trees.

Neal stood facing down the slope. "I missed you, too," she whispered. "I thought you were my friend. You were the first person who ever listened to me. The first person I had told so much to, and you made me feel . . ." She struggled with her tears. "You made me feel so good and then . . ."

"I *was* your friend," Rick said. They stood so close together, but he didn't dare touch her. They were so close together that if he had taken a deep breath, his chest would have brushed against the sleeve of her shirt.

"Then why did you stop calling?" she asked in a small, hurt voice. "Why did you make me feel . . . so lonely?"

"Because"—he was going to say it, and when he said it, he might wreck everything, but he had to say it now, or he'd never have the chance—"I wanted more than friendship, Neal. I wanted love. Neal, I think I love you."

She didn't move. He hardly dared to breathe. A midnight silence lay upon the land before them as he reached out and put his arm about Neal's shoulder, gently, touching her as he might a small, scared rabbit, coaxed to his finger tips, precious, natural, and wonderful. At his touch, she seemed to press against him without moving, so that they were facing each other, his arms about her as she faced up at him in the moonlight, and slowly her arms came about him, too, and she said in a voice that was quiet as the movement of a mouse through the summer grass, "I love you, too, Rick." He leaned down to kiss her, touching his lips to hers tentatively as, far off across the fields, an owl hooted, and a warm wind brought the smell of apple blossoms from the orchard.

Epilogue

The three of them stood in the corner of the supermarket parking lot waiting for the bus. Rick had his arm about Neal. Toots stood to one side, watching them. He was smiling.

"I still think you should stay," he said.

"No," Rick replied, holding tight to Neal. "I've got to go. The family expects me. I've been accepted at the college."

"Man learns as much working as he does at college," Toots said, reverting to an old argument he'd tried over the last two months while Rick had stayed on through the summer working at Uncle Toots' Carnival of Cars. He'd moved up from one mechanic of many to Ben's assistant. Toots made no bones about it; he had plans for Rick.

But Rick had plans of his own. He smiled down at Neal, tanned and relaxed beside him. Rick's plans involved going home to college and seeing his family, seeing Neal on vacations, and then, when he'd got his education and the time was right, maybe . . .

Maybe . . .

Neal and Rick didn't talk about the maybe, but it was there all the time as a golden cloud on the horizon. They knew they were both very young. They knew things changed as you grew older, met other people, learned other things, but they couldn't believe they'd ever feel any different about each other, so there on the horizon was that golden "maybe."

And Neal had plans, too. Toots had finally come to understand that she wasn't a doll or an ornament or a princess, but a regular girl. A special regular girl to Rick and to Toots, but regular. The way they both felt about Neal had come to form a strong bond between Toots and Rick, and of course, as soon as Toots understood that Rick wanted to keep Neal safe, too, Toots had tried his old cajoling way of trying to make Rick join the company and stay on in Linden.

Rick and Neal had discussed it. The result was that Rick was going off to college in Florida near his family, and Neal was going to go to a college near home.

Neal was coming down to Florida on her first break from school to meet Rick's family.

The heavy Trailways bus lumbered into the parking lot. Toots accepted defeat. He leaned over to pick up Rick's two old beat-up canvas suitcases. "I can do that, Toots," Rick said.

Toots waved him away. He took the suitcases off to where the bus had stopped, and the driver got down to open the hatch for the luggage.

Rick faced Neal. He put both arms around her. She hugged him lightly about the waist.

They'd had two beautiful months together. Rick had worked a day shift and lived at Adele's, and Neal had persuaded Toots to let her work in the office of the dealership.

"I won't say good-bye," he said.

"No, I couldn't bear that," she agreed.

Yet neither of them felt upset. They were more than friends now, and they were sure of each other, comfortable.

"I love you, Neal," Rick said.

"And I love you, too," she replied, and leaned up to be kissed.

The bus driver hooted, and Rick and Neal let go of each other, embarrassed at all the people watching. Neal went hand in hand with him to the bus. He got a back seat, the driver got in, closed the door with a whoosh, and then the bus was moving.

Rick looked out the back window. Neal stood with her father. Toots had his arm about her, and they were both smiling and waving. Rick waved. He knew he'd be back one day, and if he was very lucky and Neal was very lucky . . . maybe.

Maybe, he decided as the bus pulled out of the lot and gained speed heading for the highway south, was a lot. He could live with "Maybe."

Genuine Silhouette sterling silver bookmark for only $15.95!

What a beautiful way to hold your place in your current romance! This genuine sterling silver bookmark, with the distinctive Silhouette symbol in elegant black, measures 1½″ long and 1″ wide. It makes a beautiful gift for yourself, and for every romantic you know! And, at only $15.95 each, including all postage and handling charges, you'll want to order several now, while supplies last.

Send your name and address with check or money order for $15.95 per bookmark ordered to
Simon & Schuster Enterprises
120 Brighton Rd., P.O. Box 5020
Clifton, N.J. 07012
Attn: Bookmark

Bookmarks can be ordered pre-paid only. No charges will be accepted. Please allow 4-6 weeks for delivery.

N.Y. State Residents
Please Add Sales Tax

First Love from Silhouette

THERE'S NOTHING QUITE AS SPECIAL AS A FIRST LOVE.

— $1.75 each —

2 ☐ GIRL IN THE ROUGH Wunsch

3 ☐ PLEASE LET ME IN Beckman

4 ☐ SERENADE Marceau

6 ☐ KATE HERSELF Erskine

7 ☐ SONGBIRD Enfield

14 ☐ PROMISED KISS Ladd

15 ☐ SUMMER ROMANCE Diamond

16 ☐ SOMEONE TO LOVE Bryan

17 ☐ GOLDEN GIRL Erskine

18 ☐ WE BELONG TOGETHER Harper

19 ☐ TOMORROW'S WISH Ryan

20 ☐ SAY PLEASE! Francis

— $1.95 —

24 ☐ DREAM LOVER Treadwell

26 ☐ A TIME FOR US Ryan

27 ☐ A SECRET PLACE Francis

29 ☐ FOR THE LOVE OF LORI Ladd

30 ☐ A BOY TO DREAM ABOUT Quinn

31 ☐ THE FIRST ACT London

32 ☐ DARE TO LOVE Bush

33 ☐ YOU AND ME Johnson

34 ☐ THE PERFECT FIGURE March

35 ☐ PEOPLE LIKE US Haynes

36 ☐ ONE ON ONE Ketter

37 ☐ LOVE NOTE Howell

38 ☐ ALL-AMERICAN GIRL Payton

39 ☐ BE MY VALENTINE Harper

40 ☐ MY LUCKY STAR Cassiday

41 ☐ JUST FRIENDS Francis

42 ☐ PROMISES TO COME Dellin

43 ☐ A KNIGHT TO REMEMBER Martin

44 ☐ SOMEONE LIKE JEREMY VAUGHN Alexander

45 ☐ A TOUCH OF LOVE Madison

46 ☐ SEALED WITH A KISS Davis

47 ☐ THREE WEEKS OF LOVE Aks

48 ☐ SUMMER ILLUSION Manning

49 ☐ ONE OF A KIND Brett

50 ☐ STAY, SWEET LOVE Fisher

51 ☐ PRAIRIE GIRL Coy

52 ☐ A SUMMER TO REMEMBER Robertson

First Love from Silhouette

Tired of the winter blahs?
Enjoy an
ENDLESS SUMMER
by Rose Bayner Coming in January.

Four exciting First Love from Silhouette romances yours for 15 days—_free!_

If you enjoyed this First Love from Silhouette,® you'll want to read more! These are true-to-life romances about the things that matter most to you now—your friendships, dating, getting along in school, and learning about yourself. The stories could really happen, and the characters are so real they'll seem like friends.

Now you can get 4 First Love from Silhouette romances to look over for 15 days—absolutely free! If you decide not to keep them, simply return them and pay nothing. But if you enjoy them as much as we believe you will, keep them and pay the invoice enclosed with your trial shipment. You'll then become a member of the First Love from Silhouette℠ Book Club and will receive 4 more new First Love from Silhouette romances every month. You'll always be among the first to get them, and you'll never miss a new title. There is no minimum number of books to buy and you can cancel at any time. To receive your 4 books, mail the coupon below today.

First Love from Silhouette® is a service mark and a registered trademark of Simon & Schuster

First Love from Silhouette

Coming Next Month

A Passing Game by Beverly Sommers

As kicker and only girl on the Evanston High football team, Tobey basked in glory. And to top it all, she was on a personal kick of her own: should she run for the touchdown, block or intercept an unexpected pass?

Under The Mistletoe by Michelle Mathews

Her father was shocked, her mother astounded when a handsome stranger took Megan in his arms and tenderly kissed her under the mistletoe. But as for Megan—she rather enjoyed it. It was definitely going to be one of the better Christmas vacations.

Send In The Clowns by Marilyn Youngblood

Lita's heart was doing somersaults. She couldn't stop grinning. Her life was a circus! Now that she had met Jerry, she was dancing on a tightrope. But would he hold the net? Did he really plan to include her in his act?

Short Stop For Romance by Elaine Harper

Celia nearly flipped when she found out that her mother had hired Mark Maxwell to dog-sit while the Clinton family went off to a family reunion. Why he was just about the most attractive guy in Blossom Valley High! Now she would have a chance to get to know him.